SUCH A GOOD GIRL

EVA RAE THOMAS MYSTERY - BOOK 9

WILLOW ROSE

Published by BUOY MEDIA LLC

Cover design by Juan Villar Padron,
https://www.juanjpadron.com

Special thanks to my editor Janell Parque
http://janellparque.blogspot.com/

To be the first to hear about **exclusive new releases and FREE ebooks from Willow Rose**, sign up below to be on the VIP List. (I promise not to share your email with anyone else, and I won't clutter your inbox.)

- Go here to sign up to be on the VIP LIST :
http://readerlinks.com/l/415254

Tired of too many emails? Text the word: "willowrose" to 31996 to sign up to Willow's VIP text List to get a text alert with news about New Releases, Giveaways, Bargains and Free books from Willow.

Follow Willow Rose on BookBub:

https://www.bookbub.com/authors/willow-rose

Connect with Willow online:

AUTHOR WEBSITE:

Http://www.willow-rose.net

EMAIL:

madamewillowrose@gmail.com

AMAZON AUTHOR PAGE:

https://www.amazon.com/Willow-Rose/e/B004X2WHBQ

FACEBOOK:

https://www.facebook.com/willowredrose/

TWITTER:

https://twitter.com/madamwillowrose

GOODREADS:

http://www.goodreads.com/author/show/4804769.Willow_Rose

Books by the Author

HARRY HUNTER MYSTERY SERIES

- All The Good Girls
- Run Girl Run
- No Other Way
- Never Walk Alone

MARY MILLS MYSTERY SERIES

- What Hurts the Most
- You Can Run
- You Can't Hide
- Careful Little Eyes

EVA RAE THOMAS MYSTERY SERIES

- Don't Lie to me
- What you did
- Never Ever
- Say You Love me
- Let Me Go
- It's Not Over
- Not Dead yet
- To Die For
- Such A Good Girl

EMMA FROST SERIES

- Itsy Bitsy Spider

- Miss Dolly had a Dolly
- Run, Run as Fast as You Can
- Cross Your Heart and Hope to Die
- Peek-a-Boo I See You
- Tweedledum and Tweedledee
- Easy as One, Two, Three
- There's No Place like Home
- Slenderman
- Where the Wild Roses Grow
- Waltzing Mathilda
- Drip Drop Dead
- Black Frost

JACK RYDER SERIES

- Hit the Road Jack
- Slip out the Back Jack
- The House that Jack Built
- Black Jack
- Girl Next Door
- Her Final Word
- Don't Tell

REBEKKA FRANCK SERIES

- One, Two...He is Coming for You
- Three, Four...Better Lock Your Door
- Five, Six...Grab your Crucifix
- Seven, Eight...Gonna Stay up Late
- Nine, Ten...Never Sleep Again
- Eleven, Twelve...Dig and Delve
- Thirteen, Fourteen...Little Boy Unseen
- Better Not Cry
- Ten Little Girls

- It Ends Here

MYSTERY/THRILLER/HORROR NOVELS

- Sorry Can't Save You
- In One Fell Swoop
- Umbrella Man
- Blackbird Fly
- To Hell in a Handbasket
- Edwina

HORROR SHORT-STORIES

- Mommy Dearest
- The Bird
- Better watch out
- Eenie, Meenie
- Rock-a-Bye Baby
- Nibble, Nibble, Crunch
- Humpty Dumpty
- Chain Letter

PARANORMAL SUSPENSE/ROMANCE NOVELS

- In Cold Blood
- The Surge
- Girl Divided

THE VAMPIRES OF SHADOW HILLS SERIES

- Flesh and Blood
- Blood and Fire
- Fire and Beauty
- Beauty and Beasts

- Beasts and Magic
- Magic and Witchcraft
- Witchcraft and War
- War and Order
- Order and Chaos
- Chaos and Courage

THE AFTERLIFE SERIES

- Beyond
- Serenity
- Endurance
- Courageous

THE WOLFBOY CHRONICLES

- A Gypsy Song
- I am WOLF

DAUGHTERS OF THE JAGUAR

- Savage
- Broken

A PRETTY FACE CAN TAKE YOU PLACES YOU DON'T WANNA GO.

Right Next to the Right One *by Tim Christensen*

Prologue

WASHINGTON, D.C.

Something was off. Officer Dana Marshall, with Washington Metropolitan P.D., couldn't put her finger on precisely what it was that stirred up this unease inside her, but that was how she felt when stepping out of the apartment complex on New York Avenue with her partner of three years, George Parish. There was something in the air and a pinch in her stomach that told her something awful was about to happen.

But what?

"You wanna go grab a bite from that pizza place down the street?" George asked as they reached their cruisers parked on the street.

They had been called out to a domestic disturbance in an apartment building. A couple in the middle of a nasty divorce had been fighting when the man locked his wife out in the hallway and refused to let her back inside, even though she was only in her underwear. The neighbors called for help after she had been screaming at him and hammering on the door for about an hour. Dana and George had managed to get the husband finally to let his wife in and then spoken to both of them, taking their statements for the report and trying to mediate and make sure it wouldn't happen again. It was part of the job sometimes to have to act like a psychologist to keep the peace—at least for long enough to make it through the night without them having to be called out there again.

Dana nodded and corrected her belt. "Sure. I liked what I got there last time, the one with the garlic."

"That is a good one," George said. "Maybe I'll have that too."

Dana exhaled. She couldn't escape that odd sensation inside her that something was about to go down, something awful. She approached her cruiser and was about to get in when she paused.

Without knowing why, she lifted her gaze and looked toward the tall building across the street from them. It had a big glass façade and a rooftop penthouse terrace. Dana had never been inside the building but often admired it from the outside when driving by on patrol. She knew it was among the most expensive apartments in the D.C. area, and it was rumored that one of them was owned by Bruce Willis, even though it was never confirmed. But she did know that they were popular among the high society elite of the area and that you couldn't get an apartment in that building for less than fifteen million dollars. Dana had often wondered what it was like to be so rich you could afford to buy something like that.

"You okay?" George asked, pulling Dana back to reality. "You kind of disappeared there for a second."

She smiled and turned to look at her partner. "Yes, of course. I'm just hungry, I guess."

"It is getting late," he said and clapped his stomach. "Let's go."

Dana nodded and reached for the door when a sound made her turn her head and look toward the expensive glass building once again.

And just as she did, something moved on top of it, on the penthouse terrace. A woman screamed, and Dana let go of the car door, then took a step forward.

"What in the..."

She glared up toward the top of the building just as the girl screamed again, then tipped over the railing and fell from the sky.

Dana held her breath as she watched the girl fly through the air. It felt like hours went by as she stared at the body floating in the air, but it could have been nothing but seconds if even that.

The sound of the body hitting the pavement below made her stomach churn. Biting back bile, along with the urge to scream, she ran across the street to the body—or what was left of it—smeared on the asphalt.

Startled and barely breathing, Dana lifted her gaze again, looked toward the top of the building, and saw a man standing on the terrace, looking down at her from the exact spot where the girl had fallen.

Then she grabbed her gun and stormed for the entrance.

Part I

FOUR DAYS LATER

Chapter 1

Delta Airlines flight 5703 was circling the city below, and the captain announced that we had begun our descent into Washington-Dulles. I gazed out the window with a deep sigh, leaning my head against it. This had once been my favorite sight, back when it meant coming home—when it meant the end of a long journey and me getting back to my babies.

Today, it meant something completely different.

The plane began its descent, and the city below came closer like it was reeling me in, pulling me back.

"Coming home or visiting?" the elderly gentleman sitting next to me asked. He had been sitting very still during the entire flight and not uttered a word until now. I didn't mind. I was in no mood to chat with a stranger.

"Just visiting," I said.

"Oh, I see. And for how long do we have the pleasure of you staying here?"

That made me sigh as the plane bumped and landed on the runaway. "Should only be for a few days."

"Well, I'm sure you'll enjoy it here. Washington D.C. is a wonderful city. I should know. I've lived here all my life."

I smiled. "I'll take your word for it."

I pulled my carry-on out of the overhead bin, which was my only luggage for the trip since I wasn't staying long. I had a four-month-old child to get back to as soon as possible.

Why am I here again?

The newsstands on my way through the airport told me the reason. I couldn't escape it no matter how much I tried not to look.

MEDIA TYCOON RICHARD WANTON OUT ON BAIL: I DIDN'T KILL HER

MURDERER WANTON A FREE MAN

WANTON: I'M INNOCENT

I closed my eyes briefly, then shook my head, rushing past the headlines, wondering what kind of idiot judge sets a one-million-dollar bail for a guy like Richard Wanton. It was peanuts for a powerful guy like him, and, of course, he'd be able to post it.

The trial was set for May fifth, three weeks from now.

"Eva Rae!"

I walked out into the arrival hall and saw FBI Director Isabella Horne standing there, holding a sign with my name.

That made me laugh.

"You thought I wouldn't recognize you?" I asked as I approached her and gave her a big warm hug. "We worked together for ten years at the bureau?"

She looked down at her sign, then shrugged. "It was meant as a joke. Guess it wasn't very funny after all. How was your flight?"

I wrinkled my nose. "Bumpy and annoying. You know I hate to fly. It better be worth it. Dragging me away from my family at a time like this isn't exactly popular, just so you know it."

Isabella nodded. "It's important. You know I wouldn't have made you come if it weren't."

"I just don't understand why you couldn't tell me why you needed me on the phone?"

Isabella sighed, then placed a hand on my shoulder and pushed me to move forward. "All in due time. All in due time, Eva Rae."

Chapter 2

THEN:

"THE INTERNS usually sit in the middle over there, by the round table."

"Right there in the center? Where everyone can look at us?"

Samantha stared at the huge newsroom. It was her first day at WBC News, the place she had always dreamed of working as a child. She had only been there for about an hour and already met two of her favorite anchors and a war correspondent she admired. It was all a little overwhelming.

"Yes," the assistant producer said. His name was Walter.

Samantha smiled and nodded shyly. They approached the round table in the center, and Walter pointed at a computer. "You can sit here. This is Jacob. He's also an intern. He's been with us for three months now. Jacob, this is Samantha."

The young guy looked up from his screen and nodded. "Welcome."

Walter left, and Samantha logged onto the computer with the login they had given her, using her initials as username and then a password she created herself.

She leaned back in the chair as two journalists rushed by, coffee cups clutched between their hands. She recognized their faces from TV and felt a pinch in her stomach. Some of these people had been there for ages and were big names in the business. Sam could only aspire to be half of what they had made of themselves. Yet, she had big dreams for herself. She was going to be the next Barbara Walters or even Oprah with her own network. She wanted to be the biggest, but the road was so long and windy, and not many made it far. Yet her parents had always taught her it was important to dream big.

"You're better off dreaming of getting the world and getting half than dreaming of nothing and getting it all," her dad would always say.

"So, is it always this quiet here?" Samantha asked, looking at Jacob.

He didn't look at her. "What's that? Quiet? Yeah, sure, I guess so. Everyone is out on assignment. The closer we get to broadcast, the tenser it'll get. You'll see."

Sam turned her head and spotted the studio at the end of the room. The lamps were shut off and made the desk look way smaller than on TV. Sam couldn't believe that, in a few hours, she'd be sitting inside the newsroom while they aired the news from over there.

It was almost too much to take in at once.

Samantha grabbed her phone and texted her best friend, Natasha, whom she had known since Kindergarten. She had been the one to keep pushing her to reach for her dreams through the many times Sam was about to give up. As a person with dyslexia, school had been hard on Sam, and becoming a journalist was far from the natural choice. But if anyone could do it, it would be Sam. That's what Natasha had always said.

I AM SITTING IN THE NEWSROOM NOW. CAN

LITERALLY SEE THE NEWS DESK FROM TV. CAN'T WAIT TO TELL YOU EVERYTHING

She put the phone down and looked at the screen. Today was all about getting acquainted with the new workplace. She had been on a course to learn their newsroom computer system and already knew her way around it, the shortcuts, and so on. Now, she logged into it and looked at tonight's rundown, the stories they were going to bring at the five o'clock news. It felt exhilarating to scroll through it—like she had access to the holiest of holies. She could see that one of the star reporters was doing a story about a leadership crisis at the University of Maryland and within D.C.'s Catholic Archdiocese after claims of abuse. At the same time, another name that she recognized was on the story of the brutal and senseless slaying of a ten-year-old boy on his way home from school.

It was insane to be able to look at this and know that in a few hours, it would all be on everyone's TV.

Sam smiled secretively while scrolling through all the stories, feeling her heart beat faster in excitement. Then she lifted her gaze, and her eyes met with those of a man who was standing at the other end of the newsroom, where he had just entered. He was flanked by several other men in suits and blue shirts, talking to him, but he didn't seem to be listening. He was staring at Samantha, and as their eyes locked, she felt a pinch in her stomach, then lowered her eyes shyly.

It was Richard Wanton. *The* Richard Wanton. CEO of the news department. And he was looking at her.

Is he still looking?

Cautiously, Sam lifted her gaze once again to see, and as she did, her eyes met his again, and now he smiled, blissfully, like he found her amusing or even charming. She wanted to lower her eyes again when he suddenly began to move.

Oh, dear God, he's coming over here!

She watched him slide toward her while his entourage followed closely behind him, clearly frustrated that he wasn't listening to them anymore.

"And who do we have here?" he asked and stopped by her desk.

Sam could barely breathe. She had read about Wanton in the newspapers and seen his picture a million times in magazines, but now he was standing right in front of her, looking down at her, smiling, asking her who she was.

Was this guy for real?

Wanton tilted his head, waiting for an answer. Sam rose to her feet. She was fiddling with her hands. She could barely find the words to say since she really wanted to impress him. Somehow, she managed to stutter:

"I...I'm Samantha Durkin. I...I'm a new intern. It's actually my first day here."

That made him laugh. Sam didn't quite understand what was so funny, but his entourage laughed along with him.

"Okay, Miss Durkin. Welcome. We are pleased to have you."

"Th-thank you."

He nodded again and sent her one last smile, then turned around on his heel and left, his people following him, trying to keep up with him. Samantha felt her heart knock against her ribcage and could barely breathe as she watched him walk away.

"I can't believe that just happened," she said as she finally managed to sit down again. "I can't believe that was Richard Wanton. He's a lot more handsome in real life."

Jacob barely lifted his head from his computer.

"Wow," Sam said, blushing. "I think I need to call my friend and tell her. She's never going to believe that I actually met Richard Wanton."

Sam grabbed her phone and left the desk with it pressed against her ear.

"Nat. You'll never guess what just happened."

Chapter 3

There was a light knock on the door, and a head poked inside Isabella's office. I had thrown my weekend bag in the corner and sat in a chair, waiting for her to reveal to me what was so darn important that I had to come all this way.

"I thought I heard rumors you were in town," the voice said.

I turned to look up and spotted my old colleague, Timmy Gardner. I smiled widely and got up to hug him. He held me tight and lifted me slightly off my feet. Timmy was a big guy, six feet four and packing two hundred and fifty pounds, and next to him, I felt small for once.

"How the heck have you been?" he asked, grinning. "It's been forever."

I exhaled.

"Yeah, I heard about the divorce and that Chad passed away," he said. "I am so sorry for your loss."

I nodded. "Thank you. How's Virginia?"

"Just fine and dandy. We decided to separate last year during Covid lockdown. She still lives in the house with the kids while I got a small place downtown."

I placed a hand on his shoulder. "I'm sorry to hear that."

He shrugged. "What can you do? We had grown apart and being together full-time during the lockdown reminded us of that. It was probably for the best."

"It still hurts."

He nodded. "Yeah, well...has Isabella given you the details?"

Isabella shook her head. "Not yet. I was just getting to it."

I gave him a look. "You're on this case?"

He nodded, smiling. "Yup. But I'll let Isabella fill you in. I'll come back later. I just couldn't wait to say hi."

That made me smile. Timmy was such pleasant company; I was almost looking forward to working with him again. Only almost because I wasn't quite sure what this was all about. Isabella was being so secretive; it made me slightly nervous. There was something she was hiding, or at least hesitant to tell me. The question wasn't as much what it was, but why.

"I'll meet you in the interrogation room," Timmy said. "As soon as you're both ready."

"Is the subject ready?" Isabella asked.

He nodded, and they exchanged a look. Timmy's eyes grew serious.

"You haven't told her?"

"As I said, I was just about to when you came in."

My heart started to pound. "Tell me what?"

I stared at Isabella, whose eyes avoided mine. Timmy gave her a look.

"She's gonna find out at some point," he said. "Just say it, for crying out loud."

"Tell me what? This is getting very old. Isabella?"

She nodded, then finally looked up and met my eyes. "Maybe it's best if you see for yourself."

"See what?"

Isabella rose to her feet, grabbing the file and putting it under her arm. "You better come with me."

I followed her out the door and down the hallway of my old workplace, beginning to feel annoyed with her.

"Why do I have a feeling I am about to regret ever coming here?"

Chapter 4

Rachel McBeal stared at the TV in her kitchen, barely breathing. The sound was muted, but it still had her full attention. On the screen was the face of a man who had kept her awake the past few nights. Beneath his handsome smile, it read:

RICHARD WANTON LEAVING PRISON TODAY

Rachel stared at those piercing blue eyes on the screen until they cut to a live feed. A female reporter was standing in front of the courthouse downtown, her colored lips, which had recently been filled, moved weirdly as she spoke and pointed at the building behind her, just as someone walked out. The reporter now rushed toward the entrance, holding out the microphone just as Richard Wanton walked outside, flanked by men in suits. He covered his head with his jacket, and the cameras flashed, and reporters crowded him, only held back by the police officers protecting him.

Rachel watched as he was rushed to his car and helped inside, then took off, leaving the clamoring journalists behind.

Rachel didn't need any sound on her TV to know exactly what was going on. But she did need to breathe, and right now, she wasn't.

She leaned forward against the counter, then gasped for air. Her heart was beating so fast in her chest that she couldn't calm down. She dropped to her knees, her torso shaking heavily, gurgling sounds leaving her mouth.

"Mom? Mom? Are you okay?"

It was her teenage daughter, Marissa, who had walked in just in time to see her mother fall to her knees.

"MOM?" she shrieked.

Rachel tried to speak but didn't have enough air. Marissa grabbed her phone. "Dad? Dad? I think something is wrong with Mom. I think she might be having a heart attack or something. All right. I'll call nine-one-one."

Marissa got off her phone, then dialed. Rachel heard her talking with desperation in her voice. Rachel wanted so badly to be able to comfort her daughter, to tell her she was going to be all right, but she couldn't because she suddenly wasn't sure she was going to be all right. The panic inside of her, the shaking anxiety, wouldn't ease up. It held her in such a tight grip; she couldn't move. All she could do was focus on breathing, and yet it still felt like she was being strangled, like she was choking on the very air that was supposed to keep her alive.

"Yes, yes, um seventy forty-five Macarthur Street, yes, okay."

Marissa was crying, speaking through sobs.

"Please, tell them to hurry, please!"

Marissa hung up, then wiped her tears away with her sleeve. She knelt next to Rachel, who was breathing raggedly, wheezing, feeling like her airways were slowly being closed.

"It's okay, Mom. They're on their way. They'll be here soon, just...please, just don't die on me. I can't live without you; do you hear me?"

Rachel clasped her constricted chest as her throat closed up further, and she could no longer pull in air. She reached out her hand for her daughter. In the same second, her eyes rolled back in her head, and she lost consciousness. Her daughter's screams disappeared as she was pulled into oblivion, and there was nothing but peace in the deep darkness.

Chapter 5

"I take it you've followed the details in the Richard Wanton case?" Isabella asked me as she led me down the hallway. I nodded and smiled at an old colleague. Some greeted me with hugs, while others just nodded politely. It all looked very much the same, but there were many new faces, and that made me feel like a stranger. I realized I no longer belonged there, and that was okay. This belonged to a different time in my life. And so much had happened since. I wasn't the same woman.

I nodded. "How could I not have? It's all the news talks about. I take it that's the case you need my assistance on?"

Isabella nodded. "Sort of."

I wrinkled my forehead. "What do you mean *sort of*?"

We stopped in front of a door leading to the room next to one of the interrogation rooms. Isabella used her card to let us in. She threw the file on a desk and closed the door behind us. The one-way glass was dark.

"Well, you know how he's accused of having killed a young woman, right?"

I nodded. "Yes, Samantha Durkin, twenty years old. Killed on the night of April 10 by being thrown off the terrace of his apartment. Two police officers parked below saw her fall and saw him standing there, then ran up and arrested him. It's a pretty clear-cut case."

"Except Richard Wanton has the best lawyers money can buy, and the guy says he didn't touch her."

I scoffed. "So, it was an accident?"

She nodded. "According to him, yes."

"There's a special place in Hell for guys like Richard Wanton," I said. "Please, tell me you have evidence to nail him?"

"We do have something pretty strong," Isabella said pensively. "And that's where you come in."

I gave her a look of disbelief. "Me? How?"

Isabella looked down at her feet. "There was someone else in the apartment when Samantha Durkin fell."

"A witness? That's amazing?" I looked at her. "Why aren't you more excited? Who is it?"

Isabella bit her lip. "It's a woman."

"Can she testify against him?"

"She could...if she would talk to us."

I nodded. "Ah, I see. She's scared, you think? I can't blame her. Wanton isn't someone to mess around with."

Isabella nodded. "Could be that..."

"But that's not why? And how do I fit in again?"

Isabella took in a deep breath, just as the door opened to the interrogation room and someone was brought inside by Timmy. She wasn't looking up; her eyes stayed on her feet as she sat down nervously. I couldn't see her face properly because of the bent forward head, but I didn't need to.

I had seen more than enough.

I shook my head, then took a step back. "Oh, no. This isn't happening."

"Please, Eva Rae," Isabella said.

"Nope."

"Eva Rae!?"

"No!"

"But...Eva Rae, we really need you to..."

Isabella could protest all she wanted to, but I wasn't listening anymore. I grabbed the door handle, pulled it hard, and walked out of the room with angry steps. Isabella called my name behind me as I rushed to her office, picked up my weekend bag, then left.

Chapter 6

THEN:

Two weeks into her internship, Samantha was invited to a conference, along with most of the reporters at the network and their bosses. They stayed at the Grand Hyatt, where there was a dinner and an afterparty with an open bar. Samantha sat with the other interns at their table during dinner, but as the night progressed and people got more and more drunk due to the open bar, she soon moved onto the dance floor. First, she danced with one of the older reporters who had asked her. Samantha could feel the alcohol in her blood as she moved, and she felt light and was having the best time ever. People at the network were so nice and a lot of fun. She felt so lucky to be a part of this family. And that's what they said it was—that the network was just like a family. They took care of one another.

She felt eyes on her, then turned to look and spotted Richard Wanton. He was standing, leaning against the bar, watching her. Samantha sent him a smile, then continued her dancing, feeling how his eyes followed her every move. She danced with one of the anchors, Jimmy Howell, and he swung her around till she got so dizzy she almost had to throw up.

"Come on, one more dance," he said as a new song came on. He was pulling her arm, but she pushed him away.

Samantha shook her head, laughing. "I need to take a break."

She staggered away from the dance floor, laughing yet feeling so dizzy she was afraid she was going to get sick. She leaned against the bar, then found a stool and sat on it. Samantha wasn't used to drinking this much.

She hid her head between her hands for a second when she felt someone brush up against her, and she looked up.

It was Richard Wanton.

He grinned. "You all right?"

Samantha nodded and smiled. "I'm just not used to drinking this much. I think I need to hit the sack soon."

He stared at her, his eyes looking deep into hers.

"That's probably not a bad idea."

Samantha nodded. "Yeah, I think I'll call it a night."

She was about to walk away when Richard Wanton leaned toward her, placed a hand on her thigh, and whispered in her ear.

"My hotel room is 103. I'm gonna take a round and say goodnight to some people. Wait fifteen minutes, then come to my room."

He pulled back, winked at her, then turned around and left. Samantha remained seated on her stool, wondering if she had heard him right or if she had just been hallucinating.

Did he really tell me to come to his hotel room? Richard Wanton?

Samantha swallowed. She had a crush on the man back when he used to be an anchor, and she watched him every night on the news. He was handsome, and she was definitely attracted to him. But come to his hotel room? That was a little much. He was married; she knew that. But she had also read in the tabloids that they weren't doing so well—that they believed they were heading for a divorce. Could he be genuinely interested in Samantha?

She shook her head and ordered a vodka shot from the bartender. She watched Richard as he said goodnight to some of the other bosses, shook their hands, then sent her a glance as he left.

Come to my hotel room.

He had really said that, right? She couldn't have misheard him, could she? No. How else would she now know the room number?

103.

Samantha got her vodka shot, then downed it, feeling the burn as it went inside. She put the glass down on the counter.

What do I do?

Samantha weighed her options. What could she do? Could she pretend like she didn't hear him? Could she just not go? But then she risked that he'd be mad at her. He might have her moved to another department or even fired. Would he destroy her chances in this business? He was, after all, a powerful man.

She shook her head. No, she couldn't go to his room. This wasn't something she did. She simply couldn't.

Samantha glared in the direction of where Richard Wanton had disappeared, then looked at her watch as the minutes passed, approaching the fifteen-minute mark. Her stomach was turning, while she secretly wondered:

Do I even have a choice?

Chapter 7

I made it back to the hotel and threw my tired body on the bed with a deep sigh, scolding myself for being so stupid. This had been a total waste of my time. I should have known. Of course, there was a reason for Isabella's secrecy, for her not telling me who it involved. I shouldn't have trusted her. It was my own fault.

I opened my laptop while lying on the bed, then looked through flights back to Florida, trying to find the soonest one home. Unfortunately, I couldn't get any until the next day, so I was stuck in D.C. for the rest of the day.

Just my luck.

My phone was vibrating on the bed, but I didn't pick it up. Isabella was trying to get me to come back, and she was the last person I wanted to talk to. I was so angry at her right now; I wasn't sure I would ever speak to her again.

My phone screen lit up and told me I had a voice mail. I grabbed a bag of peanuts I had bought in the Orlando airport to keep my stomach from growling, then started eating while staring at the display.

Did I want to hear the message?

No. You know what she'll say. She'll use all her persuasive powers to convince you to come back. Don't fall for it.

I ate some more peanuts, then turned my focus to the computer screen instead. Then I grabbed my phone and looked at a text I got from Isabella:

I KNEW YOU'D REACT LIKE THIS. THAT'S WHY I DIDN'T TELL YOU. COME BACK, PLEASE. SHE ASKED FOR YOU. SHE'LL ONLY TALK TO YOU.

I sighed, then wrote:

NOPE. NOT GONNA DO IT.

I stared at the words on my screen, then deleted them. If I engaged in a conversation with her, she'd only think I was easing up on her. She'd only convince me, and I really didn't want that.

I put the phone back down, and it vibrated again. This time, it wasn't Isabella. It was Olivia, my oldest daughter.

I picked it up.

"Hi, sweetie. What's up? I think I may be coming home earlier. It turned out they didn't really need me after all."

"Mom," Olivia said. She sounded so serious, and I suddenly saw a ton of scenarios in front of my eyes, involving the deaths of several of my children.

"Is something wrong?" I asked, trying not to panic.

"Yes, something is wrong, Mom," Olivia said. "I just spoke to Tristan; you remember him?"

I swallowed. My voice was getting high-pitched as I answered. I knew what she was getting at.

"Of course, I remember him."

"Why won't you help her? Why won't you help his mom?"

I exhaled, then walked to the window and looked out at the town in front of me. I had once loved living there; this had been my town. Now, I felt so estranged from it. It was evident to me that I didn't belong here anymore.

"You know why," I said in almost a whisper while rubbing my forehead. "You, of all people, should understand that."

"She's in trouble, Mom. She's scared."

I closed my eyes. Those were the exact words I didn't want to hear. I didn't want to feel sympathy for the woman. I didn't want to think of her as a real person with feelings. I was fighting it with every fiber of my being.

"She was in the apartment when that guy pushed the girl over the railing," my daughter continued. "That's what Tristan told me. She's scared to be an accomplice to murder; don't you understand that? That's why she only wants to talk to you. What happened to you, Mom? You usually always help people who need it?"

I cleared my throat and nodded. "I do. But not this one. Not her."

"You have to, Mom. For Tristan. If you can't do it for her, then do it for him or me. He is my friend."

"But she... she ruined our lives, Olivia."

My daughter went quiet on the other end.

"Still, Mom. She needs your help. How can you refuse her that? It's one of the things I admire so much about you. That you always believe that people are entitled to a second chance."

Seriously?

"That's not fair, Olivia."

I hung up, then threw the phone on the bed, feeling awful. How was it that your teenage daughter always knew how to get to you? How did she always know which buttons to push? How to make you feel like the worst person in the world?

"I'm a good person, dang it."

I finished the bag of peanuts, then went to the mini bar and grabbed a soda to wash it down with and opened a can of pecan nuts and a chocolate bar.

Then, I called Isabella.

"If I say yes to this, the FBI pays my consulting fee and my expenses too, do we agree? And I plan to order room service a lot."

"Deal, Eva Rae." Isabella paused, then said: "Thank you for doing this. I know it must be hard on you."

"Hard doesn't even begin to cover it," I said and filled my mouth with more nuts and crunched them. "The woman had an affair with my husband for an entire year without my knowledge, and then Chad left me for her. Hard doesn't even come close to how this feels. I'm not sure any word suffices."

"You're a saint," Isabella said. "For doing it anyway. I mean it."

That made me laugh. "I'm not quite sure I can live up to that. Let's talk once this is over and see if I've been able to do it without strangling her with my bare hands."

Chapter 8

No words were leaving her lips. Even though she felt her lips moving, no sound seemed to come out between them. Meanwhile, the doctor and her husband were standing by her bedside, deep in conversation.

"J-Joe?"

Finally, the sound of her voice echoed off the barren walls, and the two of them stopped their conversation.

"Rachel! You're awake."

Joe approached her bedside and grabbed her hand in his.

"W-what happened?"

"You had an...episode," Joe said. "You fainted."

"Marissa?" she said and suddenly remembered her worried daughter's screams in the kitchen right before everything went dark.

Joe squeezed her hand. "She was hungry, so I told her to go to the cafeteria. She should be back in a few minutes."

Joe stroked her hair gently. "We were so scared."

The doctor stepped closer. "Your pulse suddenly plummeted, and we struggled to get it back up."

Rachel wrinkled her forehead. "But...what...is it my heart?"

The doctor shook his head. His lips grew narrow. "I have seen this before, and..."

"What?" Rachel asked, feeling terrified.

"They believe you had a panic attack," Joe took over.

"Excuse me?"

Joe squeezed her hand even tighter in his.

"Have you been under a lot of stress lately?" the doctor asked.

Rachel tried to think, then shook her head. "Not more than usual. I mean, I only work part-time, and my daughter is a teenager, so no nothing more than I normally do."

The doctor nodded. "Well, you need to figure out what caused this, so I'd recommend you start seeing a therapist. Something triggered this reaction in you, and we need to make sure it doesn't happen again."

Rachel nodded. "O-okay."

The doctor smiled, then shifted on his feet before he left. Joe sat on Rachel's bedside and looked into her eyes while touching her cheek gently.

"I am so sorry. I didn't realize you were in distress," he said. "You need to tell me these things. I can do more at home."

Rachel smiled and nodded. "I'm fine. I promise."

Joe kissed the top of her hand just as Marissa came back into the room, a big smile on her face.

"Mom! You're awake."

They hugged, and as they did, Rachel suddenly remembered what she had seen right before she passed out. Her eyes grew wide, and she felt her heart rate go up rapidly. She felt dizzy and had to close her eyes to compose herself.

"Mom?" her daughter shrieked.

Rachel felt her hands shaking as she watched the images of Richard Wanton leaving the courthouse over and over again, breathing raggedly.

"Rachel, are you okay?" Joe asked. "Do we need to call a nurse?"

Rachel closed her eye briefly, pushing the images away, hiding them deep down where she couldn't reach them. It was where they had been for years, so it had to be possible to keep them down there and close the lid.

"I'm okay," she said, her voice trembling. "I just need a second."

Rachel forced a smile and raised her gaze to look into the deeply worried eyes looking down at her.

You can never tell them. They can never know.

She grabbed her daughter's hand in hers, then looked into her eyes, making sure she listened.

"I'm fine. Really."

She managed to calm them down while everything inside her felt like it could explode at any second. She tried to push the emotions back, to hide them away as she had done for so many years, but for some reason, it was like they wouldn't stay there anymore. It was like one of those jack-in-the-box toys that once it had popped open, it was impossible to close the lid again. No matter how much you struggled and fought the darn thing, the stupid clown just wouldn't fit back inside, and the cover wouldn't stay closed, leaving you stuck with the ugly clown face constantly grinning at you.

Chapter 9

Kimmie was already sitting in the interrogation room when I got there the next day. We were watching her through the surveillance camera in the corner.

"So, you just want me to talk to her?" I asked. I had been lying awake all morning, wondering if there was any way I could still get out of this. No one would blame me for running away; I knew that much.

Except for my daughter. Except for Olivia. And I couldn't let her down.

"Yes. We need her to tell the story. She's our star witness in the case against Richard Wanton, and what she says will play a central part."

I looked at Isabella standing next to me. She was a woman in her mid-fifties, yet still stunningly beautiful. She wore that black suit and high heels like no one else. I sure couldn't pull off an elegant outfit with the amount of grace that she did.

"Otherwise, no pressure?" I said with a chortle.

Isabella shook her head. "None whatsoever."

She handed me a file, and I read through it. Kimmie had to be dying in there, but that didn't move me.

"Is this all you have?" I asked, looking up at Isabella, baffled. "This is the entire case on Wanton?"

She nodded. "I'm afraid so."

"But...it's nothing. You have two police officers who say they saw him standing on the rooftop deck after the girl had fallen. There were a couple of fingerprints and hairs from him on her clothes, but that can be explained away by him being with her before she fell. There's no proof that she was pushed. You'll never get him convicted based on this. A guy like Wanton who has the best lawyers money can buy?"

Isabella nodded again. "Tell me about it. Now, you understand why I so desperately need your help."

"And Kimmie hasn't told you anything useful?" I asked, skimming through her statements.

"All we know is she was in the apartment when Samantha Durkin fell to her death. She says she didn't see anything, but we believe she did."

I shrugged. "So, you think I can get her to say more?"

Isabella nodded. "She asked to speak to you. She said she didn't trust anyone else. We believe she knows a lot more than what she has told us, and hopefully, she'll share it with you. There are a few things that don't seem to add up."

"Like what?"

"She says she was in the bedroom when the girl fell to her death, so that's why she can't say if he pushed her. She told us she was struggling with putting her shoes back on while the officers who came to the apartment tell us she wasn't wearing her shoes. She was barefoot, and her shoes were found on the couch in the living room. She says she barely knew Samantha, but still, she knew that she had recently had an abortion. Things like that."

"Are you considering charging her?" I asked. "With accessory?"

"We're considering it if she won't tell us more, yes," Isabella said.

I looked at Kimmie on the screen, and my heart dropped. The woman had broken my marriage, and I was angry with her, but she deserved a chance. I felt a pinch in my stomach at the thought of having to face her again after all that had happened. I really didn't want to.

"Okay, and so once I get her entire statement, hopefully, a useful one, then I'm off the hook, right?"

Isabella nodded. "That's the deal, yes."

I looked at my phone to make sure my family wasn't trying to reach me. Angel, my four-month-old, was smiling at me from the picture on my background, and my heart melted. Gosh, I missed her so much.

"Let's do this," I said and closed the file. "If all goes well, I should be back with my baby later tonight."

Isabella grabbed my shoulder and made me look at her.

"Be compassionate, Eva Rae. Please. We need her to get to Wanton. Without her, he'll walk. Compassion, Eva Rae, do you hear me? Be the nicest that you can."

Chapter 10

THEN:

HER HEART WAS BEATING SO FAST. She stared at the door to the hotel room, 103. The hallway was spinning as she felt how drunk she was. She had taken a few shots while making her decision in the bar. She had thought she'd feel better about it as she approached the door, but she didn't.

Yet she lifted her hand and knocked.

The door swung open, and there he was—the handsome Richard Wanton, who could make or break a career. He was in his boxers, smiling. He was well-trimmed even though you could tell that he was starting to get what Samantha's mom would lovingly call a muffin-top.

At least he's good-looking. Twice your age, yes, but still handsome.

He looked her up and down with a grin, then grabbed her arm and pulled her inside gently. He held her head between his hands and lifted her chin, then looked deeply into her eyes. She felt herself shiver.

He leaned forward, still holding her head between his hands, then pressed his lips against hers, pressing her back up against the wall behind her. The aggressive move made her shriek lightly, but that only seemed to encourage him further. He let go of her head, then started to undress her, pulling off her top and bra. Then he paused and admired her bare breasts, his head slightly tilted, a hungry look in his eyes. He then bent forward, grabbed her skirt, and pulled it down to her ankles. Gently, he lifted her feet one after the other so he could get it off completely. Then he grabbed her panties and slowly pulled them down, leaving her standing completely naked in her high heels in front of him.

Samantha wanted to cover herself up and moved her hands to do so, but he stopped her, shaking his head with a *tsk*.

"Don't. I want to see you."

Then he pulled back, grabbed a cigarette, and lit it. Samantha could barely breathe as she stood there in the middle of the hotel room, naked, him watching her body while smoking.

Then, he smiled, his eyes narrowing.

"You're gorgeous; do you know that?"

That made her blush. No one had ever called her beautiful before. The few guys she had been with had been drunk out of their minds and fumbled in the darkness. No one had ever seen her naked like this or admired her body.

"Absolutely stunning," he added, blowing out smoke.

Richard Wanton put out his cigarette in an ashtray next to him, while Samantha didn't dare to move. He approached her, then knelt in front of her, grabbed her strapped high heeled shoes, and started to unbuckle them. He took them off one after the other, and she was now standing with her bare feet on the floor.

Richard Wanton then grabbed her hand, kissed the top of it, and pulled her toward the bed.

Chapter 11

I hesitated for just a second, took in a deep breath, and braced myself for what I was supposed to do before opening the door.

Be the nicest that you can.

It was easy for her to say.

Kimmie looked up, and our eyes met across the small barren room. There she was, the woman who had stolen my husband and destroyed everything we had built together. As always, she looked gorgeous with her unnaturally long legs, and blonde hair pulled back in a ponytail. Her big deer-like eyes stared at up me, her mouth slightly gaping as if she wanted to speak, but the words were frozen in her throat. I remained in place, just stood there, holding my breath, fighting my anger.

It was safe to say it wasn't a pleasant moment.

"Eva Rae," she finally said.

I moved forward, threw the file on the table, my eyes avoiding hers, then sat down. Without looking up, I opened the file and looked at the first page. Then, I folded my hands on top of it and finally lifted my gaze to meet hers.

"Kimmie Vanderspool. Do you understand why you're here today?"

She stared at me. I was barely breathing. I thought about the many times she and Chad had been at PTO meetings together, about the fundraiser they had worked on together to raise money for the new playground at the school. I thought about the bake sales and the multicultural nights they had both volunteered for back when our kids were much younger. Had they flirted? Had they known already then?

Kimmie nodded. "Yes."

I looked down again. "Good."

"Listen, Eva Rae...I..."

"Agent Thomas," I said. "That's Agent Thomas to you."

She formed a disappointed look on her face, then nodded. "Yes, yes, of course."

"Good."

Silence broke out between us while I fought my urge to scream. I wanted to yell at her, to ask her how on earth she could have done what she did, ask her how well she slept at night.

"Ev...I mean, Agent Thomas," Kimmie finally said. "I know you must think it's odd that I asked to speak to you, with our...um...history and all..."

"That is putting it mildly, but yes," I said as I lifted my gaze and met hers. "I did find it odd you'd ask for me of all people."

Her shoulders slumped. "I knew you'd probably say no, so I am really glad you came after all. It's just that...well, I know you. Or I feel like I do. Our kids were friends, remember? And I did enjoy getting to know your other children when Chad and I were...when we were together. So, I thought that even though...we have been through...um...a lot, maybe you'd say yes; maybe you could help me out. I know I don't deserve it..."

"You're darn right you don't," I said a little louder and rougher than anticipated. I stared at her, breathing hard, trying to stop my nostrils from flaring, so she wouldn't notice just how angry I was.

"I just..."

Kimmie stopped, and tears piled up in her eyes. I stared at her, refusing to feel sympathy for her. She sniffled, then continued, leaning forward and speaking in almost a whisper.

"I really need your help now. There is no one else I trust to tell my story to."

Chapter 12

"Let's take it from the beginning," I said after taking a few deep breaths, making sure I was calm enough. Sitting face to face with Kimmie was tougher than I had expected it to be. I wanted to rip her head off. I wanted to yell at her, tell her I believed she was the actual scum of the earth, that there was a special place in Hell for women who did what she had done to me.

But this was not the time. Of course, it wasn't. Besides, I wasn't interested in listening to her make excuses. What she did wasn't something that could be solved with a simple "I'm so sorry." We both knew that. But, of course, she'd try to justify her actions. I just wasn't willing to hear it.

"It says here that when Officer Marshall and Officer Parish came into the apartment and arrested Richard Wanton, they found you in the bedroom, sitting on the floor. You told them you hadn't seen what happened, but you heard the scream."

Kimmie nodded. Since I had last seen her, she had lost weight, and it showed on her face with visible cheekbones and sunken cheeks. She'd have to be careful not to lose any more weight since she'd end up looking older than she was.

"Yes, that's true."

"Let's go back a little bit. What were you doing in Richard Wanton's apartment in the first place?"

I cleared my throat and leaned back in my chair, waiting for her to take over. She stared at the edge of the table for a few seconds before she finally opened her mouth to speak.

"I...I know him from years ago," she said, fiddling with her fingers on the table.

I looked into the file. "You are a journalist?"

She nodded. "I worked as a reporter at WBC News."

"And Richard Wanton worked there as well?"

"He was the news director back then. It was fifteen years ago."

"He was your boss?"

She nodded. "Yes. He hired me fresh out of college. Gave me my big break."

"Would you say you have a good relationship with him?"

She paused, then said:

"He taught me everything I know."

I looked at her, noticing that she didn't answer my question. I wondered if it was deliberate. Was she afraid of saying that she liked him? Maybe I'd think she was his accomplice? That she helped him kill the girl? Or that she might be protecting him? Was she trying to hide her involvement somehow?

It was too early to tell.

I tried again:

"But it's safe to say that you two were friends since he invited you to his apartment, am I right?"

A long pause.

"I owe him everything. He kick-started my career."

Again, she avoided the answer. I decided to let it slide—for now, at least. I sighed. This was getting annoying.

"Kimmie, I need you to give me a little more here. All I know is that you were in Richard Wanton's apartment when Samantha

Durkin was killed. We're desperately trying to figure out what happened. Can you enlighten us?"

She nodded pensively, biting her lip.

"I'm getting to it. Just be patient with me, okay?"

Chapter 13

I was beginning to think I was wasting my time. I kept thinking about Angel and how badly she had to miss me. She wasn't used to being away from me, and I felt awful for leaving. But I had to admit that I truly enjoyed getting some uninterrupted sleep last night.

I rubbed my forehead and leaned forward. Kimmie drank water from her cup. I desperately needed some more coffee.

"I met him a few weeks ago in a bar," Kimmie finally began. "He was out with friends, and I was out with a couple of girlfriends when he came in. They were all laughing and having a great time. They had been to some fundraiser dinner somewhere else in town, then stopped the limo at a bar to get a beer on the way home. That's what he told me when he spotted me sitting there and came over. Then his assistant called me up out of the blue a week later and invited me to dinner. I was told he wanted to talk about me getting back to working again. I was naturally thrilled. I have been struggling these past few years, doing freelance writing for different magazines, but I really wanted to get back into television. It was my dream, and it burst when I was pregnant with Tristan."

I looked up at her. "Okay. Now, we're getting somewhere. Did you go to the dinner?"

She nodded, then looked away. "I did. On the night when...when the girl was..."

She paused and sniffled, her eyes still avoiding mine. "Okay, let's dial back a little. You went to dinner. Where was it?"

"At Mastro's. I had salmon; he had a steak."

"Expensive place," I said and wrote it down. "And what did you talk about?"

She lifted her gaze. "Mostly old times back at WBC News. Old stories about our former colleagues. He then asked me if I was interested in going back to work in television because he had an opening in his news department. It was the position of an anchor and would be a good fit for me, he said. He knew that was my biggest dream back then, so naturally, I was very excited when he started to tell me about it. I wanted it so badly."

"Badly enough to sleep with him to get it?" I asked, leaning forward.

Her eyes met mine. Hers seemed desperate.

"I'm sorry," I said. "For jumping the gun, but they did find you in his apartment, in the bedroom, so I just assumed that he..."

"There's always a catch, isn't there?" Kimmie said, her eyes tearing up. "Especially in this business. It's just the way it is, the way it has always been."

"And you saw this as your last chance at getting your career back," I said.

She swallowed, then nodded. A tear escaped her eye, and she wiped it away fast. "I'm not getting any younger. This was my last chance. After he had talked about this anchor position for a very long time, he suddenly leaned forward, grabbed my hand in his hand, and said: 'The job is yours within twenty-four hours if you'll have it.' I distinctively remember how my heart was pounding with joy as the words fell. 'Oh, but I do,' I said naturally. And then he said: 'And within those twenty-four hours, you'll also have slept with me.' That's when everything crashed inside me. He went to the bathroom, and I was dying inside, trying to make the decision. I'm not seeing anyone; I haven't been since...well, Chad left me to go back to you...so that wasn't an obstacle. And no one needed to know, right? I mean, I could get it over with and then start the job the following day and forget all about it. This could change my life, both for my son and me. The money was amazing, and the job was everything I ever wanted. It wasn't that big of a deal, I thought. I'd be fine."

"So, you went with him."

Kimmie looked away, then nodded. "When he came back from the bathroom, he reached out his hand and asked if I was ready. I grabbed it and went with him to his limo, then let him take me to the apartment. Yes. That's how much of a slut I am. But I guess you already knew that."

Chapter 14

Kimmie was sobbing, her eyes lowered, looking at her shoes. I refused to feel sorry for her. She didn't deserve it.

I cleared my throat, then looked down at the file again. "You went back to his apartment to seal the deal," I said. "And then what happened?"

Kimmie swallowed. She sniffled, and I grabbed the tissue box and handed it to her. She wiped her nose and eyes.

"It's just so...embarrassing," she said, almost hiccupping from crying.

I exhaled and rubbed my forehead. She was crying heavily now. I leaned forward. "Listen, Kimmie. We've all done things we regret, okay? If it's any help, I don't think less of you for telling me this. I don't think you could fall any lower, so..."

That made her chuckle between sobs.

"Point taken."

She took another tissue and wiped her eyes, then looked up at me.

"So, what happened?" I asked again.

She took in a deep breath. "We took the elevator up to his penthouse apartment, and as we walk inside, I saw the girl."

"Samantha Durkin?"

"Yes."

"You knew her name?"

"No. I didn't at this point. She told me later."

"Okay," I said, writing it down. "So, she is already in the apartment when you get there?"

"Yes. She's sitting on the couch and looks up as we enter. Her eyes are big and fearful, but Richard just smiles."

"Did you say anything?"

"I looked at Richard and asked, 'who is she?'"

"And what did he say?"

"'Does it matter?' That's what he said, with a grin, of course. And then I was about to back out when he grabbed my arm and told me to come closer. And then he said he wanted us all to have sex. He wanted me to...well, be with the girl...um Samantha, and then he'd watch and later join us."

"A threesome?" I asked.

Kimmie nodded, then sniffled again. "I...I didn't know what to say. I have never done anything like that before. I'm a good girl, darn it. This wasn't what I had said yes to. It was too much. I told him so, and then Samantha started to say the same. She didn't want to either. Then he told us we were both applying for the same job and that he would make his decision based on our performance that night."

I stared at her, suppressing the urge to act appalled.

"What did you do?"

"I should have left."

"But you didn't."

Kimmie shook her head, her eyes tearing up again. "I needed the job; I really did. It would change my life and Tristan's. We were struggling. I don't know if you know what it's like when you don't know if you'll have enough money to feed your child next month? The life of a freelancer is tough. I haven't been able to find a steady job since the hours are unmanageable, but now that Tristan is older, I could finally accept one with strange hours. It might sound odd, but I didn't feel like I had a choice."

"And the girl? Samantha? What did she say?"

Kimmie, struggling to keep calm, bit her lip.

"She...she wanted to leave."

"Did you know her?" I asked.

Kimmie shook her head. "Never seen her before."

"You sure?"

"Yes. She was way younger than me. My guess is she worked for him in one of his news stations."

I nodded. "She did." I flipped a page in the file. "She was an intern. But it says here that you said that you knew she had an abortion recently. How can you know that if you didn't know her?"

Kimmie went quiet for a minute, her eyes flickering.

"She told me that while we were in the apartment."

"That's something pretty serious to talk about in a situation like this," I said.

"Wanton was on the deck outside smoking, and we got to talking. She was super scared of being pregnant again."

I stared at Kimmie, biting the side of my cheek, not quite grasping this. I decided to let it go.

"That's also when she told me she'd go tell him that she had decided to leave," Kimmie continued. "She told me she'd tell him she wasn't having it, that she was done, and it didn't matter if she got the job or not. She didn't even want it this way. I admired her guts as she got up and walked out to him. I had never heard of anyone standing up to Richard Wanton before."

"Then, what happened?"

Kimmie paused. I could tell this was hard for her. Her breathing was rapid now, her nostrils flaring lightly.

"It's okay, Kimmie. You can tell me. You can trust me. I might be angry with you for what happened with Chad, but you can still trust me."

She looked up at the small round camera placed in the ceiling in the corner of the room. "Is anyone else listening in?"

I nodded. "Everything is being recorded, yes."

"That's what scares me. Not you, but those that are listening in."

I nodded in reassurance. "I understand that. But I know these people. There are two of them, and both have been my colleagues and friends for years. They're good people. I trust them. I can vouch for them."

Kimmie locked eyes with me. I could tell she was struggling.

Then, she nodded, her head heavy.

"Okay. I trust you, Eva Rae." She shook her head. "I mean, Agent Tho..."

I reached out my hand to stop her.

"It's okay."

She smiled. It came off as anxious.

I leaned forward and folded my hands on the table. "Kimmie. What happened to Samantha?"

"She...she walked out to him on the terrace," Kimmie said, her voice breaking. "And then...I...I watched them from inside, arguing."

"And then what happened?"

Kimmie lifted her eyes and met mine again. She was crying now.

"Then he...he grabbed her arms and yelled. I couldn't hear what he said, but his face was really close to hers, and she was scared, very obviously scared, and she sort of scrunched down, and then she tried to get out of his grip. She pulled away, but he...he pulled her back forcefully, and then he...he..."

She stopped and looked down at her fingers.

"He what, Kimmie? What did he do?"

She lifted her eyes and met mine again. The look in them told me what she was going to say before the words left her lips.

"He pushed her."

"He pushed her?"

Kimmie nodded. "He pushed her toward the railing, and then he pushed her, so she slipped over it. I saw him do it and heard her scream. It was the strangest thing. One second, she was there, then the next...gone. Poof, just like that. It was like she had never existed. It felt so surreal."

"And what did you do?"

Kimmie took in another deep breath. "I was completely paralyzed. I stood there, staring at the window, and then I ran to the bedroom and hid in there. I locked the door, afraid he'd come for me next. I had my purse and was looking for my phone to call for help. But I never did because then the officers burst in. They had seen it happen from the street, and they arrested him. I was lucky they came when they did. There's no telling what he might have done to me if they hadn't come right when they did."

Chapter 15

"That's it."

Carol dropped the fork onto her plate. She clenched her fists and bit down hard, speaking through gritted teeth.

John Savage looked up at her, surprised at this outburst. They were in the middle of dinner, salmon quiche, prepared by Lola in the kitchen. There had been a long silence between them when Carol suddenly broke it.

"I want out."

John tilted his head. "What do you mean you *want out*?"

She closed her eyes briefly and made an annoyed sound. "Out. I want out of this, of us. We've been married for twenty years, John, and I can't do it anymore."

John stared at her, still chewing. "What are you talking about?"

"I'm sick of this, of being here, of being married."

John shook his head. Where was this coming from all of a sudden? He reached out his hand to touch Carol's.

"Honey, what on earth is going on?"

She pulled her hand away. She lifted her arms and spat as she spoke. "I'm done. You need to listen to me, John. I am leaving you."

"But...why? What did I do?" he asked desperately.

Carol sent him a look that could kill.

"Like you don't know."

"I'm trying my best here, Carol."

She exhaled deeply, then rubbed her forehead. "I...I just can't take any more of this. I want out."

"Carol, honey. I know there have been issues...in the past, but I thought we worked through them. There hasn't been... anyone else for a very long time. I have been good. I thought you knew."

She looked at him, her brown eyes cold and harsh. Then something happened in them as they met his. They eased up, and she had a gentle expression on her face.

"There really hasn't been anyone? Honestly?"

He shook his head. "There's only you."

She exhaled and eased her shoulders, narrowing her eyes. "Really? Because it was driving me nuts to have to worry constantly... I mean, every time you receive a text or someone calls, I can't help thinking that it's...well..."

John smiled and reached out his hand toward Carol. This time, she took his in hers. "I promise you, Carol. There's no one."

"That's so good to hear. Thank you, sweetie," she said and finished her wine. He poured her some more while she breathed easier.

"Say, how about we go away for the weekend, huh?" John asked, smiling gently at Carol. He had loved her since they met twenty years ago, and he knew he had put her through so much. She didn't deserve the way he had treated her.

"To that place up north you love so much?"

Carol's eyes grew wide, and a smile spread across her face.

"The one in Martha's Vineyard? You know I love that place."

"That's a deal, then," he said. "I just need to go push back a couple of meetings; give me a second."

Carol nodded, her eyes gleaming as she looked at him. John left the dining room and went to his office, where he grabbed his cell phone and called a number.

"Hi, it's me. Any news about our little friend?"

John nodded as the person filled him in, worry starting to nag at the pit of his stomach. He hung up, then dialed another number, his hands getting sweaty.

"She's talking," he said. "It's bad. We need to do something."

Chapter 16

THEN:

THE ALCOHOL BUZZ was wearing off. Samantha glared at Richard Wanton, who was still naked on the bed, smoking another cigarette while watching her get dressed. It was late, and the sun about to rise outside. She had to get back to the hotel room she shared with another intern before she woke up and started to ask questions. Samantha felt strange. She couldn't really put it into words, but as the effects of the alcohol slowly wore off, the feeling of having screwed up became more and more evident.

What was she doing?

"Anyway...I'll just be..." she said and pointed toward the door.

Richard Wanton put out his cigarette, then slid down from the bed and walked to her. Samantha felt embarrassed and lowered her eyes as he leaned over and kissed her on the cheek while placing both hands on her shoulders, then took in a deep breath like he was smelling her.

"I'm gonna have a lot of fun with you," he whispered in her ear. He smelled like a mixture of sex and cigarettes.

"W-what do you mean?" she asked.

That made him smile, his blue eyes narrowing as he studied her. He caressed her cheek gently, then grabbed her by the neck and pulled her closer till his face was right in front of hers, and she could smell his breath. A chill ran down her spine.

"I mean, I want to have sex with you in my office, in my car, and the basement beneath the TV station."

Samantha's eyes grew wide. He was still holding her head, and she could barely move. She didn't know what to say to him.

"I...I didn't even know there was a basement beneath the TV station?" she said, then thought it was the stupidest thing in the world.

That made him chuckle. He looked into her eyes, and it made her feel weird. What was this? What was going on?

"I'll show you," he said.

"I...I should..." she said and pointed at the door behind her again. She desperately wanted to leave now.

Richard Wanton let go of her, then kissed the top of her hand while Samantha felt her heart race in her chest.

She turned around and reached out for the door, then he sprang forward and opened it for her, then held it open. Samantha smiled awkwardly, feeling such deep confusion as she was about to leave.

Then he grabbed her by the shoulder, leaned forward, and whispered in her ear:

"I'm gonna screw you so hard; you won't be able to walk for two weeks."

Hearing this, Samantha gasped and looked at him. As he closed the door behind her, still smiling like they were now sharing a secret, she felt like she was going to be sick. She clasped her mouth and ran down the hallway, found her hotel room, fumbled with the keycard, and hurried inside. She closed the door behind her. Then she ran for the bathroom and threw up.

Chapter 17

"I think I have all that we need," I said and closed the file. I glared at Kimmie across the table. Her eyes lingered hopefully on me. We had spent hours going over her statement, again and again, to make sure it was bulletproof.

"So, what happens next?" she asked, her voice shaking lightly.

"It's out of my hands from here on," I said. "But now they'll use your testimony to try and build a case against Wanton. Hopefully, there'll be physical evidence from the apartment backing up your testimony and then...hope..."

Kimmie shook her head. "That's not what I meant."

I paused and looked at her.

"I meant what happens to me?" she continued.

I rubbed my forehead. "I'm not sure I'm the right person to answer that. But I take it you go home and then..."

"No!"

I wrinkled my forehead. "What do you mean by *no*?"

"No, I'm not going back home. There's no way."

"But...but what about..."

"It's too dangerous. I can't go back."

"So, what did you have in mind?"

She reached out her hand and grabbed mine. The touch felt awkward, and I wanted to pull it back but didn't.

"I know Richard Wanton. He's a powerful man. He's gonna try and get rid of me. I need protection," Kimmie said.

"I'm sure that Director Horne can get you into a protection program; it really isn't my specialty. Let's go talk to..."

Kimmie held onto my hand as I tried to get up. She shook her head again, her eyes desperate.

"No, please. I don't trust them. I don't trust anyone here. They could all be in his pocket. He's got friends everywhere. I fear he's preparing to have me killed as we speak."

I exhaled. "Kimmie. It's okay. You can trust us. I promise you."

"Will you protect me?"

"Excuse me?"

"I only trust you. Can you protect me?"

I looked at my phone on the table, then thought about Angel, feeling a pang of deep guilt for being away. I shook my head.

"I'm sorry. I don't do that. I'm a profiler. Besides, I have a baby to get home to."

Kimmie sank back in the chair. I could see the fear in her eyes, but I ignored it. Instead, I grabbed the file, rose to my feet, and looked down at her.

"Listen, Kimmie. You'll be fine. The FBI has great programs for protecting witnesses. They know what they're doing."

"I just really wanted you to be there," Kimmie said.

I smiled compassionately. "I understand. But look at me. I recently had a baby. I am in no shape to protect anyone. I truly do believe they have other people here that are better at that than me."

"And you're sure I'll be safe with them?"

I leaned forward, then nodded. "Absolutely. Trust me on this, Kimmie."

Part II

ONE WEEK LATER

Chapter 18

Joe stood by her bedside, sighing deeply. Rachel had her back turned away from him, hoping he'd leave soon.

"Are you planning on staying in bed all day...again?" he asked.

Rachel closed her eyes briefly, then opened them again. Two days ago, she had been driving down her street when suddenly it had hit her, hard. It was like this big black hole had opened up beneath her and sucked all life and hope out of her. Then she had started to cry. Her torso shaking heavily, she had let the tears gush down her cheeks. It had become so violent that she had to park the car on the side of the road to be safe. There she had sat for two hours, unable to move. She had been crying, bawling her eyes out, unable to stop. And she had been crying ever since. All the day before, she had been unable to get out of bed. She had simply laid there, hour after hour, staring at the window, crying. Joe had to make dinner when he came home from the office late, and she hadn't eaten anything all day. She simply had no desire to. All she wanted was to stop crying, but the tears kept coming.

This morning, she had woken up at the same time as Joe, but she was just lying there, unable to move as he got himself ready.

"I'm leaving now," he said. "I'm taking Marissa to school. In case you care."

Rachel wanted to say something; she wanted to nod or at least somehow acknowledge that she had heard him, that she appreciated that he took over the way he did when she was unable to. But nothing came out; she had no strength even to turn around and look at him. Instead, she felt the tears come again and closed her eyes, hoping she could somehow force them back inside, or at least that they wouldn't leave her body if she kept her eyelids shut. But it was hopeless, and she felt her cheeks get wet.

Oh, no. Not again!

"Rachel? Are you even listening?"

I am. I hear you. I just don't know what to say. I just can't get the words out. But I do hear you, Joe. I'm just too sad to answer.

He exhaled behind her, and she felt the weight of a hand land briefly on her shoulder before she heard the footsteps leave, and soon the front door slammed shut as they both left.

Rachel laid still in the bed, the pillowcase below getting soaked. She wondered how long it was going to be like this. She had barely made it home that day when it started. She had fought just to be able to hold it back enough for her to make it back, and as soon as she parked in the garage, it had overwhelmed her. She stayed inside the car for half an hour after she had parked, simply crying.

When it finally subsided slightly, she had dragged herself inside, crawled into bed, and not left it since. She was beginning to wonder if she ever would. For every hour that passed, the weaker she felt, and the sadness only grew in strength. What was this? What was going on with her? Would she ever be herself again?

You have to pull yourself together. You have a family. You have people who count on you, who need you. Why can't you just stop? You're so weak, such a fool!

Rachel took a deep breath and tried hard to lift her head from the pillow, but no matter how much she wanted this, it didn't happen. She simply couldn't move, and now the tears welled up in her eyes again. If only she knew why she was crying. If only she had an explanation, something to tell her family when they came back home. But she didn't. All she could feel was this deep hopelessness, this sense that she wouldn't be here tomorrow, that her life was over.

And then she had a thought. She suddenly wondered if her family wouldn't be better off without her. What if she ended it here and now? All it took was a jar of pills. She'd swallow them all and go to sleep forever.

Suddenly, for some reason, it felt like a solution to all her problems.

It was a way out.

Chapter 19

She felt safe—at least as close to safe as she could get. Kimmie had spent an entire week in what they called a safe house. And she had Tristan with her. That was the critical part, that they were together and that they were safe.

Ever since she had told Eva Rae Thomas everything, she had been struck by this deep fear that she had somehow also put a mark on her own head. But so far, everything had remained calm, and she and Tristan felt like they were protected. They had two big guys with them inside the apartment, armed to their teeth. Both seemed like nice guys, but they mainly kept to themselves, insisting on remaining professional. When Kimmie asked them if they wanted to eat dinner with her and Tristan, they said no, and if she asked them if they wanted to play a board game or a card game, they politely refused as well. And Kimmie understood. Their job was to guard them and nothing else.

But being locked up in a small space like this for an entire week with nothing to do but watch TV or play games was getting a little tiresome. Kimmie wasn't allowed to have any contact with the world outside, so no cell phones, no iPad, or computer. She and Tristan were both completely cut off from the world outside. And it was driving her slightly insane. It wasn't fun for Tristan either. How do you tell a teenager that he can't be on his phone? That he couldn't be in contact with any of his friends? It was like torture for a sixteen-year-old boy.

"Can't we go for a walk?" he asked. "I really need to go outside."

Kimmie shook her head. "Not yet. We can't risk anyone recognizing you."

Tristan grumbled and threw himself on the couch. He turned on the TV and zapped through the channels till he found some ridiculous show that he could watch. Kimmie sighed and joined him. She wondered how long they'd have to live like this. She knew she had asked for it; she had asked to be protected, but still. This was too much. And they still hadn't told her what would happen once she had testified in court. Would she be able to live her life again? Could she go back to normal? Or had she ruined everything? She knew she wouldn't be able to work as a reporter again. That much was certain. Richard Wanton had friends everywhere, and no one defied him. Not even if he went to jail. But that was the price she was willing to pay as long as the guy got what he deserved.

"I'm going to the bathroom," Tristan said and got up.

Kimmie watched him walk past her, then felt awful for him. She wasn't certain he'd ever get to see his friends again. What if they had to start over somewhere else?

It wasn't fair to him.

Kimmie sighed as she heard the bathroom door close, then looked toward the two big guards, Jimmy and Brad, who were sitting by the door. Brad closed his eyes briefly, then opened them again and blinked. Kimmie chuckled at this. It had to be the most boring job in the world, she thought. She almost felt sorry for them.

That was when the lights went out in the entire apartment.

Kimmie shrieked, shocked, then realized she was being silly. It was probably just a power outage that would be fixed soon. There was nothing to worry about.

Not until she heard the door being kicked in and two rapid shots being fired.

POP-POP

That's when she knew.

She wasn't in a safe house.

She was in a death trap.

Chapter 20

I had Angel on my hip while making her bottle with the use of only one hand. I poured in water and then added the formula powder before shaking it. Angel was cooing on my hip. I loved the sounds she was beginning to make. It was so adorable. I was enjoying my time with her so much.

I shook the bottle, then sat down in a chair and fed her.

I looked at her little face, the chubby cheeks, and cute nose. Looking at her while she drank her bottle made me almost forget how many times I had to get up the night before. I was beginning to wonder if she'd ever sleep through the night. My mother kept telling me just to let her scream through the night as she had done with Sydney and me, but that was never my style. I simply couldn't stand hearing my child cry and believed she needed me. So what if I didn't get much sleep?

The milk spilled down her cheek as she let go of the bottle again, and I pulled her up to burp her over my shoulder. Angel fussed a little, and I gave her the bottle again, and she emptied it. Her eyelids grew heavy, and I could tell she was fighting the urge to sleep. I took her upstairs, then put her in her bed, turned on the monitor, and left while Angel slowly dozed off.

Then I walked downstairs and poured myself a cup of coffee. I grabbed my phone and was going through my texts when Christine, my fourteen-year-old, called me.

"You're in school," I said, picking it up with a swift movement. "You don't call me when you're in school."

"I'm not feeling well," Christine said. "Can you pick me up?"

"What do you mean you're not feeling well?" I asked suspiciously. "What's wrong with you?"

"I have a stomach ache."

I rubbed my temples, feeling a headache approaching. "Again? You don't sound sick, Christine. Are you sure you're sick?"

"Mom, I am not feeling well. Aren't you listening?" Cristine snapped. "You never listen to me."

"Do you think you have a fever?" I asked, thinking she was making this up. Christine wasn't very happy about school lately and had stayed home twice last week with a stomach ache. I had a feeling she was just trying to get out of school. I had done the same thing in middle school, so I knew the drill. Middle school was the worst, but it was something you just had to get through. I had tried to explain that to her, but apparently, it hadn't sunk in.

"No, but my stomach hurts."

I sighed and looked at the clock. Angel would sleep for another hour. At least I hoped so. I couldn't leave her, and I didn't want to wake her up either. I had just gotten her to fall asleep, and she'd end up crying the rest of the day if she didn't get her nap.

"You'll have to wait. I just put Angel down. When she wakes up, I can pick you up, okay?"

"What?" Christine squealed. "You can't be serious!"

I exhaled. "It's the best I can do. I can't leave the baby. Don't you think you can wait an hour?"

"NO! I can't wait an hour, Mom. My stomach really hurts!"

I took in a deep breath to calm myself and not let her sense of drama get to me. It wasn't like she was dying here, even if she wanted me to think so.

"I understand that, but maybe you can walk home then? It's not that far."

"What? Walk home? You can't be serious? Don't you understand what I am saying? I'm sick, Mom!"

"I'm sorry, sweetie. It's the best I can do right now. Maybe go to the clinic. Nurse Patricia can let you rest there."

She scoffed. "I'm not going to the clinic, Mom. I wanna go home. Can't Grandma look after the baby?"

"She's in Orlando today, I'm afraid. It'll take her an hour to get back. I'll come as soon as I can."

"Why is everything about the baby? Why can't it ever be about me?"

"Christine, that's not fair. You know I do the best I can."

"Yeah, right," she said. "Thanks for nothing."

Then, she hung up. I looked at the display, then shook my head at her. She was such a teenager these days. Everything was so dramatic. I just couldn't let it get to me. I had been through the same with Olivia when she was that age. It was going to get better. It would pass. She was going to become my sweet girl again one of these days.

Right?

I put the phone down and grabbed my coffee, enjoying the peace and quiet. I knew it wouldn't last long. Having little ones and teenagers in the house at the same time wasn't exactly easy. All my attention was on the little one, and everyone else felt left out constantly. Even Alex, who was eight now, was beginning to show jealousy toward Angel. He was struggling with not being the youngest and cutest anymore.

I exhaled and drank more coffee when my phone vibrated on the counter. Thinking it was Christine again, I picked it up, feeling annoyed, but then I realized it wasn't her number on the display.

It was Isabella Horne.

"Now, what?" I asked.

"I have some bad news, I'm afraid."

"It usually is when you call. What's going on?"

She sighed. "There was an attack on the safe house where we kept Kimmie and her son."

I almost dropped my coffee cup out of my hand. "An attack... what...what does that mean?"

Silence followed.

"We lost her; we lost Kimmie, our star witness."

Chapter 21

She had to think fast, and much to her surprise, that's exactly what she did. Kimmie jumped at the sound of the shots being fired, then ran for the bathroom, thinking only of protecting her son.

She used her shoulder to knock open the door, then hurried inside, sliding sideways on the slippery floor, panic erupting inside her. Sparse light from the moon outside came in from the window in the bathroom, and she could see a shape she assumed had to be Tristan lying on the floor.

"Mom?" he shrieked. "What's happening?"

Kimmie heard turmoil from the living room and guessed whoever had fired those shots was coming for them. She had to move quickly.

Kimmie glanced up toward the window, then crawled up on top of the toilet to reach for it. She could hear footsteps as they strode across the wooden floors in the living room. Kimmie struggled to breathe properly as she pushed away the plastic plant placed on the sill, found the handle, and managed to push the window open. She glanced out and saw the fire escape right below.

"Come," she whispered to Tristan and jumped down. "Hurry."

Tristan rose to his feet. He stood on the toilet to reach the window, then slid through it. Kimmie watched him go through, heart pounding in her chest when she heard movement close to the door leading to the bathroom. She gasped and turned to look. She couldn't see anything in the darkness but still sensed someone was there. Heart throbbing in her throat, she crawled up on the toilet, her hand slipping, so she almost fell. A noise at the doorway made her gasp and look. As she did, the light from the window fell on a shadow, a big shadow, moving closer and on the gun that was pointed at her.

Move, Kimmie! Don't just stand there!

She reached up and grabbed the windowsill, then got herself pulled up. She groaned and grumbled as she fought to push her head out the window.

"Mom!"

Tristan stood below her on the fire escape, looking up concerned. He reached up his arms to grab her and help her through. But as he did, Kimmie felt a cold, gloved hand grab her leg. The hand was strong and clenched down hard. Panic rushed through Kimmie, and she stared at her son below her.

"Tristan!"

The grip on her calf tightened, and she felt a jerk so strong and forceful, she couldn't fight it. She was pulled back inside.

"MO-O-O-OM?"

Her son's scream rang through the air as she disappeared back into the bathroom, slamming her head on the windowsill on the way and then on the top of the toilet. Kimmie screamed in pain and fear, holding up her hands to protect her face as she was being dragged back onto the floor, then let go.

She looked up to see the face of her attacker but could only see the shape of it. The roughness and the strength told her it was probably a man.

"Please," she said as the light hit the gun and she saw it was pointed at her, and she imagined the finger moving on the trigger.

"Please. I have a son who needs me."

Chapter 22

"Is she...is she...?"

I was holding the phone in my hand while my entire body shook. So many thoughts rushed through my mind in this second; most of them had to do with Kimmie and how she had begged me to protect her.

And then I refused.

"We found the bodies of the two guards inside the apartment," Isabella said. "But we never found Kimmie or Tristan. The window in the bathroom was left open, and the fire escape was right below. There was blood on the floor and a cracked pot with a plastic plant in it on the tiles—smashed. The pieces had blood stains on them, and we're having it analyzed.

I lifted my eyebrows. "You're telling me they escaped?"

"That's what we don't know," Isabella said. "We have no idea where she might be. No matter what happened to her, chances are she won't take the witness stand after this. We lost her."

"But at least she's most likely alive," I said, feeling a rush of adrenaline go through my body, then being replaced with great relief. I sat down on one of my kitchen chairs, holding my forehead, calming myself by repeating this information over and over again in my mind.

They didn't find her body. That means she's probably alive. And Tristan too.

"Could she have been kidnapped?" I asked.

"We have no way of knowing what happened," she said. "But it's possible."

"Were there any surveillance cameras in the building or nearby?" I asked.

"We're looking into that now. We had cameras outside the apartment and down by the building entrance, surveilling the front doors, but they are both gone."

"Really? But then you should have recordings on the hard drive of the person that took them down at least?"

Isabella sighed. "Unfortunately, it's not there, no."

"How is that possible?"

Isabella went quiet, and I figured she had asked herself that very question a lot of times too.

"What are you doing now?" I continued.

"Trying to find Kimmie and her son," she said. "We have put out a search, but we're trying to keep it low key, so the media doesn't find out we lost our only witness. But we have to find Kimmie somehow. We need her if we're going to take down Richard Wanton. We can't do it without her testimony. Anyway, I just figured I should tell you. You're somewhat invested in this case and in Kimmie as well. And then, well...of course, in case she contacts you, please let me know, okay?"

I promised her, then hung up, heart aching in my chest. I stared out into the street, wondering what happened to Kimmie, where she was now, and whether she was safe. I felt awful for refusing to protect her, for not being there when she needed me, even though I hated her guts. She had so specifically requested me to help her, and then I had said no. It didn't make me feel good. To be honest, I hadn't really believed she was in danger. I should have known that a guy like

Wanton would do anything to get rid of her. But how he had gotten to her was beyond my comprehension.

As I thought about this, I suddenly spotted my ex Matt's police cruiser as it drove up in my street and parked in my driveway. I wondered for a few seconds if he was coming to pick up Angel but then remembered he wasn't supposed to have her till Friday.

I stared at the cruiser as the door opened, and Christine stepped out, slamming the door, then rushing toward the house. I almost dropped the phone in my hand, then hurried to the front door as she came through.

"What on earth do you think you're doing?" I asked as her face poked inside. She looked at me, startled. "You're involving Matt now?"

She shrugged. "He's still on the list of people who can pick me up at school. And you weren't coming."

I placed my hands on my hips. "Christine. Matt is no longer my boyfriend. He doesn't live with us anymore. You can't just call him and have him pick you up."

She looked up at me. "Why not?"

"Are you even sick?"

"I told you. My stomach hurts."

"I don't think that's enough for you to leave school early. You're getting too many absences lately. You'll get in trouble."

She shrugged. "So what? It's not like I'm learning anything useful anyway."

I gave her a look as she hurried past me and up the stairs. I walked outside to Matt, who was still in the driveway, rolling his window down when seeing me.

"I am really sorry," I said. "She shouldn't be calling you."

"It's okay," he said. "I wasn't doing much anyway. It's been a couple of quiet weeks around here. I was happy she thought of me. I miss her and the others too."

I sighed. "That's sweet. But it won't happen again. I promise."

He nodded. "Okay. I'll see you Friday when I pick up Angel?"

I nodded, crossing my arms across my chest. I was about to walk away when I paused, then turned around.

"Actually?"

"Yes?"

"Could you take her tomorrow? Something has come up. I have to go away for a few days."

He smiled. "Sure. I'd love a couple of extra days with my daughter. It's no problem."

"Great. I'll have my mom come over for the big ones."

"What's going on? Where are you going?"

I paused for a few seconds, realizing I hadn't thought this through. It just felt like the right thing to do at this moment.

"I'm going back to D.C. Something has come up, something urgent."

He smiled again. There was a sadness to it. He was still angry about me breaking up our engagement. I knew he was, even though he was trying to hide it.

"Always trying to save the world," he said with a sliver of bitterness to his voice. "You don't change, do you?"

I shook my head.

"I'm not planning to, no."

Chapter 23

Rachel took the pills down from the cabinet, then grabbed her glass of water. She poured out the pills in her hand, an entire handful of them, then stared at them, thinking how strange it was that such small things could be so deadly.

It's for the best, Rachel. They're better off without you, and you know it. This way, you don't have to cry anymore; you don't have to be such a burden. It'll be all over, and then you won't have to feel anything anymore. Can you imagine? Never feeling this pain ever again?

The small voice in the back of her head was right. She couldn't bear to feel like this anymore. She couldn't keep crying. She couldn't keep feeling this profound sadness that wouldn't leave her alone. It was too much.

Rachel felt the tears as they welled up again, and she let them run down her cheeks as she readied the pills in her hand. She sniffled, then stared at them, making the final decision.

No way back now.

She parted her lips, closed her eyes, and lifted the hand with the pills, leading them toward her mouth, and shuffled them all inside.

She then grabbed her glass of water and lifted it toward her lips when her phone lit up next to her with a message. Rachel didn't know what drove her to look, but she did, and as she saw the message on the display, the words jumping out at her, she dropped the glass with water on the tiles, then hurried to the sink and spat out all the pills. They spurted into the sink while she coughed and spat, making sure each and every one of them was gone.

Crying, she leaned over the sink before washing the pills down the garbage disposal, sobbing, her torso shaking heavily. She then reached for the phone and opened the message, reading through it, her hands shaking heavily, her breath getting stuck in her throat.

WE NEED TO TALK, it said. YOU'RE NOT ALONE. I KNOW THIS BECAUSE IT HAPPENED TO ME TOO.

A picture of Richard Wanton accompanied the text. Seeing this, Rachel gasped for air. She had to lean on the counter as her knees gave way underneath her. Rachel stared at the picture, feeling sick to her stomach. It was a strange sensation since it usually was one you'd want to avoid, but she welcomed this nausea. It was the first thing she had felt that wasn't sadness in a very long time. For once, she was feeling something, something real.

She was feeling anger.

Another text popped up on her phone as she was still looking at the photo sent to her in the first one.

MEET ME IF I CAUGHT YOUR INTEREST. WE'LL TALK. FIVE O'CLOCK ON WEDNESDAY.

Then a second went by, and a pin in Maps was sent to her, showing her the location for a restaurant downtown. Rachel looked at the jar of pills on the counter. Half of them were still left inside of it. She grabbed it and looked at it, then threw them in the trash. For the first time in weeks, she wasn't ready to give up. She had one more fight left in her, and that had to be taken care of first.

Chapter 24

I landed in D.C. right around noon the next day and drove my rental car straight to the hotel. I threw my suitcase on the bed, then pulled out my laptop. I opened Instagram on my phone, then scrolled through Kimmie's feed, stopping at each and every picture to study it. I had done it before and knew she hadn't posted anything in about six months, but I kept wondering if there was something in her old photos that might give me a hint or a direction to go in. There were a lot of pictures of her and Chad from the time they lived together.

After he had left me for her.

It filled me with disgust. And anger. So much anger that I hadn't allowed myself to feel in a long time.

We had children together, Chad. Dang it. We were a family.

Now, Chad was gone, and I had no one to direct this anger at except for Kimmie. I felt it rise in me and grow stronger and stronger with every picture I looked at.

What am I doing? I hate the woman, and now I am trying to help her?

I put the phone down with a deep exhale, then rubbed my forehead, closing my eyes, realizing I had no idea why I had come back. What was I trying to do here? Get closure? Forgive her?

I stared at the articles on my computer screen. I had been reading everything I could find about the murder of the young girl, Samantha Durkin, in Richard Wanton's apartment. I wondered about her and who she was. The media had written tons about her, and what most people—like her colleagues, family, and friends—said about her was that she was "such a good girl." I chewed on those words. It was something we often said about young girls, but what did it really mean? That she got good grades in school? That she worked hard, maybe even volunteered at an animal shelter? What? And why was it important for a girl to be good? Would we say the same about a boy? If Kimmie ended up getting killed, would we say the same about her? That she was such a good person? I probably wouldn't. She slept with my husband for crying out loud. And what if I died today in some tragic death? Would they say the same of me?

Probably not, I decided and chuckled. I knew my mother thought I had made a mess of myself, and Matt was so angry with me it was like he almost hated me. I believed I had done a lot of good in my life; I had saved a lot of people, and I had helped put a lot of bad guys behind bars. But had I done good? It depended on who you asked, didn't it?

I grabbed my phone again and went back to Kimmie's Instagram profile, encouraged by a thought that had suddenly struck me. I remembered when Chad had just left me for Kimmie. I had been obsessed by checking her profile and going through her pictures, seeing what she and Chad were up to and how *oh-so-happy* they were. I would look at her in all those pictures and feel sick. I would be so jealous that I wasn't as pretty as her and tell myself that's why he left me—because I wasn't blonde and didn't have long legs like she did—because I wasn't skinny and fit like her. It was self-torture, but we do that to ourselves sometimes, right?

I know I did. I was very good at torturing myself.

I found an old picture, then paused and clicked on it. It showed

Chad and Kimmie in front of a sign. His arm was around her, and she looked up at him with loving eyes. The picture still made me feel sick, just as it had before, but I had never realized just how much love there had been in her eyes when she looked at him.

Could it be that Kimmie was really in love with Chad? There were always two sides to every story, and if you asked Kimmie, maybe she had just followed her heart. She had fallen in love with the wrong man.

My man.

Chapter 25

THEN:

THINGS WERE CALM, and more than a month had passed since Samantha slept with Wanton in his hotel room. She was getting on with her life and career and beginning to feel like maybe she could just forget it ever happened. She had been drinking and done something stupid, but maybe no one ever needed to know. Perhaps she could put it behind her.

Maybe.

She didn't know if she was just being paranoid, but she felt like people looked at her differently when she walked around the TV station, especially in the newsroom where all the reporters and the anchors sat. Sometimes, she'd felt like they'd look at her weirdly or stop talking as she entered the room. Some smiled strangely at her, like Mitt Paige, the most prolific anchor at the network. Before they went away to the conference, he had never noticed her or looked in her direction, but now, for some reason, he kept saying hello to her and smiling, almost grinning as they passed one another in the newsroom or the hallways. She even caught him turning his head and checking her body out as she walked past him once.

It made her feel slightly uncomfortable if she was honest. Because why had that suddenly changed? Was it because they knew what had happened?

Sam felt so embarrassed; she could barely think about it. She had told no one what happened because she was so scared of them looking down on her, of them telling her she was a fool. She hadn't even told Natasha, and she told her everything. But this, she hadn't been able to share. It was simply too embarrassing. Sam couldn't believe she could have been so stupid.

Drunk and stupid.

"Are you almost done?"

Sam looked up from her screen. Jarrett, the assistant producer of the day, glared back at her, an annoyed look on his face.

"You're running late," he continued. "You better get going."

Sam grabbed her laptop, then rushed to the edit suite, where a guy named Greg was waiting for her. She knew him a little, as they had chatted once in the cafeteria, but she had never worked with him. He was supposed to be the best, so she wasn't worried. But people said he was also a tough guy—especially on the interns.

"Glad the princess could make it," he said when seeing her rush inside. "Let's get to work, shall we? We don't have long, and with your lack of experience, we're gonna need all the time we can get."

Samantha nodded and sat down. She opened her manuscript, so she was ready. As she did, a private message blinked in the corner of her screen. The newsroom computer system had a feature where you could write direct messages to each other, and they were deleted right after you read them, so if it were from the producer, you'd better write down what he said, so you'd make sure you got the directions correct.

Samantha clicked to open the message, expecting it to be from the producer or maybe the reporter whose name would eventually be on the story once it aired.

But it was from neither of them.

It was from him. Richard Wanton.

MEET ME IN THE BATHROOM NEXT TO EDITING SUITE 10. I WANT TO KISS YOU.

Sam stared at the screen and the words blinking in front of her, barely able to breathe. What the heck was this? She couldn't leave now.

I AM EDITING, she wrote back. LATER?

NO. YOU COME NOW.

Samantha stared at the words, trying so hard to think of a way out of this. But she couldn't find any. This was Richard Wanton, for crying out loud. He was the CEO. He could ruin her life without as much as blinking.

She stared at Greg next to her, her palms getting sweaty. He was editing the first couple of sequences together on the timeline.

"Uh..."

"Yes?" he said without looking at her. He stared at the computer screen in front of him where the footage was uploaded. Sam had looked through it all and found the clips and interview bits she wanted to use, so it would be easier and faster for Greg to put it all together in the end. But she wasn't sure if what she had done was good enough—if it was sufficient.

Sam took a deep breath to gather her courage. Her heart was racing with fear. There was no way she dared to say no to Wanton.

"I...I need to...go to the bathroom real quick."

Now, he was looking at her, his weathered face folding in worry. "You think you have time for bathroom breaks? We have forty-five more minutes before the next reporter comes in here, and if you're not done, then there will be no story in the news tonight."

Samantha swallowed as another message ticked in from Wanton.

NOW.

Samantha almost jumped in her chair when she read it. She felt so anxious; her heart pounded in her chest.

"Uh...okay...but I just...I really have to go, and..."

Greg sighed deeply and rolled his eyes at her.

"All right. You're new, so I'll let this one slide. But hurry up, okay? I am not taking the fall if this story isn't done in time."

"Of course not."

"You're playing a risky game here," he continued lecturing her. "Remember, they won't give you another chance like this if you fail to make the deadline. Just be prepared for that. It's all on you if you do."

"Naturally. And don't worry. It won't be long. I promise I'll come back as fast as I can," she said, got up, then rushed out of the suite while Greg shook his head at her with a loud *tsk-tsk*.

Chapter 26

They sat at the back of the restaurant in a corner, Kimmie keeping her eyes on the plate in front of her. She was done eating, but Tristan was still working on finishing his burger. Kimmie was down to only thirty-one dollars of the cash she had stolen from the body of the guy who had attacked her in the apartment.

She was still shaking at the thought of him pointing that gun at her. She couldn't believe how lucky she had been or how brave her son had been. He had saved her by coming back through the window. He had seen the gun pointed at Kimmie, then grabbed the pot with the plastic plant in the windowsill and thrown it at the attacker. Tristan was a pitcher at the high school and a darn good one, so he had hit the man just right in the head, hard enough to make him go down. Kimmie and Tristan had then stolen his cash and run for their lives. They had hitchhiked and been picked up by a nice woman who helped them get out of town. She didn't even need an explanation. She said she could see the desperation in Kimmie's eyes and knew she had to help.

"You don't need to tell me the details, hon. I have seen that look before," she simply said, then floored the accelerator.

Now that the money was running out, Kimmie was running out of options too. There was no way she could pay for the room they were staying in, and she was beginning to consider the possibilities or the lack thereof. Would she have to leave in the middle of the night? Would they end up living on the streets?

Meanwhile, she kept her eyes and ears open for the mentioning of her name. She had seen no cops around so far and hadn't seen their faces plastered on the big TV screen above the bar, where they mostly showed baseball, but also the news. Yet, she didn't believe they weren't looking for her. She knew they would be.

Both the FBI *and* Richard Wanton.

Kimmie drank from her beer, then glanced toward her son. He was no longer a boy. In the instant he saved her life, he became a man. And what a handsome one he was. Just looking at him made her smile. She'd do anything to be able to give him his life back. It wasn't fair to have it stolen from him like this at the age of sixteen. He was supposed to be out there trying to get in contact with girls, worrying about his acne and grades. Not be with his mother on the run from the police and assassins.

What have I done to him?

Kimmie exhaled and finished the beer just as Tristan took the last bite of the burger. He looked up and smiled at her, and she smiled back lovingly like only a mother was capable of.

Kimmie avoided eye contact with anyone as they went back to their room upstairs to turn in for the night. She watched the news once more just to be certain they didn't mention her or Tristan, then turned the TV off and laid in the darkness. The inside of this room was all they had seen for several days now, and she wondered just how long she could keep this up. At some point, people were going to ask questions or ask for money, and then they would be in trouble. So far, they had just ordered food and put it on the room. Thirty-one dollars wasn't going to get them very far.

Kimmie closed her eyes to try and sleep. Sleeping was the only thing that made all this awful worry go away. If she could, she'd sleep all day, even though she knew that wasn't the solution for anything.

As she dozed off and her breathing grew heavier, she didn't even hear the person crawling up on the balcony outside their room.

Chapter 27

The streets were wet, and it was still pouring down as I drove through town. The windshield wipers on my rental car made a strange sound as they tried to keep my vision clear. The GPS on my phone told me I still had fifty miles left.

I had planned on waiting until the morning to go and was already in my bed, ready to get a good night's sleep, when I couldn't find rest. Maybe because I kept thinking about the conversation I'd had earlier with Isabella when I called her.

"Any news?"

"No, we haven't found her or the boy yet," she said, sounding more than exhausted. "And it worries me."

"I feel like there is something you're not telling me."

Isabella sighed. "We ran a DNA test on the blood we found in the bathroom and had a match."

"So, you know who tried to kill her?"

"Sure do."

"And that made you even more worried," I said. "Who is he?"

"His name is Yossi David. He belongs to one of the world's largest corporate-intelligence companies, Black Koll."

"I know them," I said. "Run mostly by former officers of Mossad and other Israeli intelligence agencies."

"Exactly. They have branches in Tel Aviv, London, Paris, and here in Washington. They offer their clients what they call 'the skills of operatives highly experienced and trained in Israeli's elite military and governmental intelligence units.' You know."

"Oh, I do know," I said and cupped my mouth. If this guy was after Kimmie or if he already had her, then we had to act fast to bring her to safety. These guys weren't joking around. They weren't only just helping to gather intelligence for those that hired them; they were also killers. I had no idea that Wanton would take it to this level, but it made a lot of sense now. It didn't make me feel better about my decision not to help her out when she asked me to. I couldn't stop thinking about the two officers that had been guarding her in the apartment. They didn't stand a chance against this guy. It was a miracle that we hadn't found Kimmie's dead body in there as well.

As I lay awake, I couldn't help thinking about why we hadn't found her body. Had Wanton wanted her alive? If so, why? Or had she gotten away by some odd miracle?

"Are you sure I can't persuade you to come back here?" Isabella had asked.

"I can't," I had lied. I didn't want her to know I was already there. I needed to be able to do my own thing first. "Kids and stuff."

"Ah, I see. Well, let me know if you change your mind. We could use your eyes on this, especially since you know her."

"I wouldn't say I know her well," I said right before I pretended I had to go, so she wouldn't start asking questions, and we hung up.

I stared at the phone, then opened Instagram again and looked at Kimmie's profile and the old picture of her and Chad.

I drove into a small town south of D.C. called White Oak, and it was like entering a completely different world with all its small quaint houses and landscape. I drove up in front of the building and parked right under the sign that I recognized from the Instagram photo and killed the engine.

Coming here was a far stretch, but it was worth a try, at least—desperate times and all that stuff.

As I stared at the dark building in front of me, I was beginning to wonder if it wasn't too far a stretch, if I had made a mistake.

And then I saw something that made me realize that not only had I come to the right place, but also at the exact right time.

Chapter 28

She didn't wake up until it was too late. Kimmie had been dreaming, a wonderful dream where she was back with Chad, and everything was perfect. She woke up with a gasp, bathed in sweat, when she realized the sliding doors leading to the balcony were open, and for one brief second, she wondered if she had left it that way or maybe Tristan had woken up and needed some fresh air.

But he was still next to her in the bed.

Then she felt the presence of someone in the room, and before she could scream and wake up Tristan, she felt a clammy gloved hand cover her mouth. She was yanked off the bed and onto the floor. She tried to kick out from underneath him as he dragged her across the carpet. Panic spread inside her as he stopped, put her head in his lap, and placed a gun on her cheek. Kimmie grumbled something beneath his gloved hand until she spotted the gun. She stared in desperation at her sleeping son. The gun had a silencer on it like the ones you saw in the movies, so chances were he wouldn't even hear it as the trigger was pulled. He'd just wake up to find his mother dead, blood staining the carpet.

Killer long gone.

He'll blame himself. He'll always wonder why he didn't wake up in time to save his own mother, how he couldn't have heard anything. He'll suffer from unbearable guilt for the rest of his life!

She tried to scream again, "Help, help me!" with the result that the attacker tightened his grip on her mouth, and as she writhed and fought him, trying to hit and kick, he pulled her head back so hard her neck cracked. As she looked up at him, panic-stricken, she saw his finger move on the trigger and closed her eyes, deciding this was it. There was no more for her here on this earth.

They had won. The bad guys had won.

Chapter 29

It wasn't pretty. I was very happy no one was around to see me climbing up the drainpipe toward the balcony on the second floor, where I had seen the guy climb up. I had a hard time pulling myself up as my arms weren't strong enough, and as I rolled onto the balcony, panting in exertion, I hurt my shoulder. I didn't have time to complain, so I got up, then cursed my bad shape before pulling out my gun from the pocket of my hoodie and hurrying inside through the sliding doors.

I made it just in time to see her lying on the floor, a man in a red baseball cap holding her, a gun placed against her head.

The finger on the trigger was moving just as I spotted them, then paused as the guy laid his eyes on me. We locked eyes for a few seconds, me pointing my gun at him.

"You let her go now, or I'll kill you."

"Mom?"

Tristan sat up in the bed.

"What's going on? Mo-OM?" he shrieked the last part as he saw his mother on the floor.

"Stay where you are, Tristan," I said, not taking my eyes off the guy I assumed only could be Yossi David, the hired killer.

"You're in a pickle now," I said, addressed to him. "Guess you wish you had killed her in the bed after all. But you decided to take her out on the floor. Maybe because you're not a bastard after all? You were thinking about Tristan, am I right? You didn't want him covered in his mothers' blood. See, it's just those small signs of empathy that trick a profiler like me. It shows me you're human; somewhere in there, there's a guy who maybe saw his own mother be killed once or someone else dear to you. Am I right?"

There was silence. Yossi wasn't moving. Neither was I. I was waiting for him to call my bluff, to realize I was just trying to win time by speaking to the small part of him that actually held empathy.

"Am I right, Mr. David?" I said, making it personal. "Or should I say, Yossi?"

He gave me a look of surprise.

"Yes, I'm not just anyone," I said. "I know who you are and who you work for. That makes me one step ahead of you."

"Mom, I'm scared," Tristan said behind my back.

"Stay where you are, Tristan!"

I lifted the hand not holding the gun to signal for him to stay back. I couldn't risk him getting caught in the line of fire should it come down to that.

Yossi stared at Tristan briefly, and I saw something in his eyes, fear, just for a brief second, before it was gone again.

"You can't kill her while her son is watching, can you?" I asked. "Because it happened to you? I can't blame you, Yossi. We all have a weak spot. As I said, it makes you human."

Yossi's eyes glared out from underneath his red New York Yankees baseball cap, and I could tell I was getting to him.

"You know why the guy that hired you is trying to get rid of this woman?" I asked. "Because she watched him murder someone. A young woman. He threw her over the railing of a rooftop deck, and she fell to her death. Only twenty years old. That's who you work for.

He wants to get rid of someone who dared to speak up. I bet your mom would have done the same, am I right? She would have spoken up about injustice. Was that what got her killed, huh?"

Yossi stared at me, his hand holding the gun still steady as a rock. Yet I saw that his right eyelid twitched slightly. Then a shadow went across his face, and something changed.

He let go of Kimmie and rose to his feet, still staring at me.

And just as I thought I had won, and a sense of relief was seeping slowly through my body, Yossi pulled the trigger and fired a shot.

Chapter 30

The gun barely made any sound as it was fired because of the silencer. Yet whatever little it was ripped through my flesh and bones. My heart stopped. I wasn't breathing. I stared, terrified at the lifeless Kimmie on the floor, then up at Yossi.

He lifted the gun and pointed it at me.

I dropped my gun, raised my hands, and took a step back.

"Please, don't shoot."

We stood like that for probably only a split second, but it felt like some very long minutes.

"MO-OM!"

The scream coming from behind me made the hairs rise on my neck. I turned to look at Tristan, who threw himself forward, then grabbed him as he approached her, holding his chest while he fought me. He was too out of it to realize he would be the next to be shot if he came any closer.

"No, Tristan."

"Mo-o-om," he continued, his face torn. "Please. No."

I heard a noise behind me, then turned and realized we were

alone. Yossi David had left—probably run out the door. I thought about going after him but realized a guy like him would be long gone by now. He had done what he came for. He had finished the job.

I let go of Tristan and let him run to his mother, then grabbed my phone and called for help. I knelt next to Kimmie and touched her throat. There was a pulse, even though it was weak. She was bleeding heavily onto the carpet beneath her. I examined her torso and found that the bullet had gone into her chest, then realized there was an exit wound in her back. That was a good sign.

What wasn't was the amount of blood gushing out of her.

I asked Tristan to pull off a sheet from the bed, then pressed it against the wound in her chest, trying to apply pressure and stop the bleeding. The white sheet soon turned red, and my fingers were covered in Kimmie's blood.

"Don't die on me, Kimmie. Come on!"

"Is she okay?" Tristan shrieked behind me while I spoke to the woman at the alarm central, holding the phone clutched between my shoulder and cheek, using both my hands and weight to apply more pressure on the wound.

"Is she going to be okay?"

The blood on my hands scared me, and I could tell it frightened him as well. There was so much of it, and it just kept coming like a flood.

Please, come now, please.

I listened for the ambulances, for sirens to bring me relief, but everything was so silent except for Tristan's heavy sobbing. The sheets were completely soaked now, my hands were bathed in her blood, and I felt so helpless. Kimmie's skin was turning paler by the second.

"Don't die on me, please, don't die! Come on, Kimmie!"

I was crying now, and Tristan screamed helplessly as he watched life seep out of his mother.

That's when I finally heard the sirens. They were still far in the distance, but they were coming closer.

I lifted my gaze and met Tristan's terrified eyes.

"Go," I said to him. "Go meet them down there. Guide them to us, so we don't waste any time. GO!"

I stared at him, tears springing to my eyes as he left, and I felt Kimmie's heart stop beneath my hands.

Chapter 31

THEN:

SAMANTHA FELT nervous as she approached the restroom. She met a colleague in the hallway and smiled awkwardly.

I want to kiss you.

That's what he had written. She could do that, right? A little kissing wasn't too bad. She could do that.

Right?

Samantha stopped in front of the door, hand on the handle, heart throbbing loudly in her chest.

What am I doing?

She wondered for a second if she could just go back—if it was even a possibility. What would happen if she did that? Would he get mad at her?

Probably.

He had seemed very insistent in his messages. She didn't dare to anger him. Besides, it wasn't like he was ugly or anything. And it was just a little kissing. It couldn't harm anything to let him kiss her. It was even a little flattering to her that a guy like Wanton liked her.

She just didn't like that it had to be in the restroom. It seemed so...well, so dirty somehow. And she also knew he was married, which made her feel bad for the wife.

Samantha looked down at her hand, then pulled the handle and opened the door. He was already there as she slid inside, praying no one saw her. He was holding a file of some sort in his hand, which he now placed on the sink before he grabbed the door behind her and locked it. Samantha gasped lightly, then felt his hand take her and pull her closer. He held her face between his hands, then put his lips against hers in a deep, demanding kiss. Samantha closed her eyes and kissed him back. His tongue filled her mouth while his hands were touching her breasts outside on her shirt.

Samantha opened her eyes and looked into his as his lips parted with hers. Then she smiled nervously. He smiled back, then reached down, grabbed her by the hips, and turned her around. He then pressed her down over the toilet, so she had to lean on it, then grabbed her skirt and pulled it up.

Samantha felt her heart rate go up as he pulled her panties down and pressed himself against her.

She wanted to protest; she wanted to tell him no, this wasn't what she had come here for. Not like this.

But it was too late. He was inside of her, pushing himself on her.

Samantha closed her eyes and focused on holding on, so she wouldn't slip and hurt herself while he did what he had come for.

Then he let go of her and zipped up his pants. She straightened up, her hands shaking as she pulled her panties back on. Wanton fixed his hair in the mirror, then grabbed his folder under his arm, gave her one last glance, then said:

"Lock the door after me. Wait five minutes after I leave before you go out. Then, no one will suspect a thing."

He then kissed her on the cheek. Samantha stood there, and not knowing what else to say, she simply nodded.

Wanton left, and she did as she was told and locked the door. As she heard his footsteps walk away outside, she put her back against the door and slid to the floor, hiding her face in her hands, hoping her salty tears would somehow miraculously wash away the humiliation.

Chapter 32

I stared down at my blood-covered hands. The blood was Kimmie's. I was sitting in the hospital waiting area while they fought for her life somewhere behind the swinging doors. The ambulance had taken her and Tristan with them and left me alone in the parking lot, covered in Kimmie's blood. They had managed to get her heart pumping again, but she had lost a lot of blood, and her chances were small.

The woman I had wished dead so many times had died between my hands. Her heart had literally stopped. And now I wished more than anything in this world that she would live.

I sniffled and leaned back in the chair. I had seen a lot of other people come and go, and a lot of eyes kept staring at me and at the blood that I didn't have the strength to wash off. I rubbed some of it off my hands, but it didn't help much. Tears ran down my cheeks, tears of frustration and brokenness.

Please, don't die. Please, don't.

I could have saved her. That's what I kept thinking about—how I messed up the entire situation. How I could have acted differently, and maybe he wouldn't have shot her. That's all I thought about—that and then what I'd do if she didn't make it. I'd have to take care of Tristan. No doubt about it.

The thought was devastating. The poor boy needed his mother.

"Eva Rae?"

The voice was Isabella's. She had come out from between the swinging doors. I looked up and met her eyes. I had called her to let her know what happened and then told her not to ask any questions until later. She shook her head. "What on earth are you doing here? I didn't even know you were in town?"

I gave her a look, then broke into tears. "Oh, Isabella. It was awful."

She sat down with a deep sigh. She grabbed my hand in hers. "I'm sorry, Eva Rae. She didn't make it."

"What?"

Isabella shook her head. "They called it about half an hour ago. They did everything they could; there were complications and..."

"You can't be serious?" I almost shrieked, cupping my mouth. "Please, tell me you're lying. Please."

She exhaled and placed a hand on my shoulder. "I'm sorry, Eva Rae. I wish I had better news. I really, truly do."

Oh, dear Lord, please, tell me it didn't happen. Please!

"And Tristan?"

"He's with her now. His grandmother is on her way. She'll take him in."

I stared at her, shaking my head slowly, refusing to acknowledge this. It couldn't be happening. It simply couldn't.

"Maybe we should get you back to the hotel, so you can get cleaned up. And then we'll get you on a flight back home to your family. You did what you could, Eva Rae. Please know you couldn't have done more."

I stared at her, my eyes filling again. "Of course, I could have done more. I could have saved her, Isabella. I failed. I completely failed."

Isabella pulled me into a deep hug, and I sobbed in her arms.

"No, Eva Rae. You couldn't. This guy was a professional. You need to let it go now. Go home and be with your children. That's where you're needed now."

Part III

ONE WEEK LATER

Chapter 33

She was the most beautiful woman in the restaurant. As Rachel entered through the glass doors, she had no doubt in her mind that she had to be the one who had contacted her. She didn't know how she knew, you could call it a hunch, but she just did.

Rachel walked directly to her table and looked at the woman with the dark hair and blue eyes. The woman smiled and nodded.

"I am so glad you could make it, Rachel. Please sit down."

Rachel pulled out the chair and slid into it. It was a nice restaurant, and she regretted wearing yoga pants. The woman in front of her was wearing a nice light red dress with long sleeves and dangling gold earrings. She looked like a million, whereas Rachel looked like she came straight from the gym, which was far from the truth. She hadn't done much exercise in months; heck, she hadn't done much of anything since she sank into this odd depression.

The waiter brought them water, and they each ordered a drink. The woman got a Cosmopolitan, while Rachel just had a glass of Chardonnay. She never dared to order drinks like that and look refined and city-like. Chardonnay was safe and one you never went wrong with.

"I take it you're curious," the woman said after her first elegant sip. "Why I have asked you to come? My name is Crystal, by the way."

Rachel nodded. She was curious.

Crystal narrowed her eyes while smiling. She leaned forward, her hands folded in front of her.

"I contacted you and asked you to come because I...or rather *we*... need your help," she said.

Rachel nodded and sipped her wine, taking bigger sips than she usually would, hoping it would calm her nerves.

"With what exactly?"

Crystal looked to the sides, then leaned forward. "As I told you in the text, I know..." she paused and looked at Rachel. "I know that... some stuff happened to you. I have been researching, looking for other...victims...women who have been assaulted and abused by Richard Wanton. Your name came up a few times during this research."

Rachel almost choked on her wine. She felt her cheeks grow warm and her throat tighten.

"I...I don't know...if..."

Crystal reached out her hand and put it on top of Rachel's. "It happened to me too. And so many others. There are many of us."

Rachel stared into the woman's eyes. She felt like crying again when thinking about Wanton and seeing him leave the courthouse, a free man again. That's what had started it all, the panic attacks, the fear, the depression, seeing him get away with it, getting away with murder this time. That's what had thrown her into almost killing herself. She simply couldn't bear it.

Rachel exhaled. "You're telling me you're gathering a group of women to take down Richard Wanton?"

Crystal smiled and leaned back in her seat, holding the stem of her pink drink lightly between her fingers.

"That is exactly what I'm saying. It's about time he tastes a little of his own medicine, don't you think? The bastard needs to be taken down."

Rachel stared at the woman, her heart pounding in her chest. Could it really be that there was something she could do to stop him? That he hadn't won after all? Even though he did walk away from the courthouse a free man? Even though the news said that the case against him was falling apart? Even though he had been on *Sixty Minutes* and told the world he was innocent and that he was the victim of a witch-hunt?

"All right," she said, nodding. "Count me in. Tell me what you need from me."

Crystal lifted her glass and clinked it with Rachel's in the air.

"To taking Wanton down."

"To taking him down," Rachel replied and smiled genuinely for the first time in many months.

Chapter 34

Angel cooed and looked up at me from my arm. I was holding the bottle, and she kept grabbing for it. I placed it between her lips and leaned back in the chair. Angel drank while looking into my eyes. There was nothing like that early contact with your child to make all your problems go away. Looking into her gaze, getting to know her, was the most rewarding thing in life, I believed.

"Who are you going to be, little Angel?" I whispered with a sniffle.

It had been a tough week to get through after Kimmie's death, and I had to fight to get myself out of bed in the mornings after what happened. But Angel kept me on my toes, which was good. Otherwise, I wasn't sure I would get up at all. I felt so strangely disillusioned.

I couldn't believe I hadn't been able to save her.

You did all you could. Those were Isabella's words. But somehow, they rang false to me. I wasn't so sure I had done everything. If I had called for help as soon as I had seen the guy climb onto the balcony? If I hadn't gone there alone?

But you didn't know he was going to be there. You thought you were just coming to talk to Kimmie, to try and get her to come back, or at least see if she was even there. You couldn't possibly have known this would happen.

I shook my head and leaned back, rocking my child back and forth gently in the chair, hoping she'd fall asleep soon. The whole story just seemed so strange in my mind. I had called and asked Isabella when they'd need my statement for the case against Richard Wanton. Because they were naturally trying to prosecute him for murdering their witness, right?

She had barely wanted to answer and told me to get some rest for now. "I'll be in touch when—and if—I need your help."

If? If?

What the heck was that supposed to mean?

A twenty-year-old girl had been killed, murdered, and Kimmie had seen it happen. And then Kimmie was murdered by hired help. All fingers pointed back at Wanton. My testimony had to play some role in this, a pretty important one, I should think. But they hadn't asked me about it at all. I knew the FBI had taken over the investigation since I had called the local police in White Oak and asked them if they needed me to come in. They told me they hadn't been allowed to touch the case at all, that FBI Director Horne had taken over immediately.

It rubbed me the wrong way somehow.

Angel let go of the bottle and closed her eyes briefly before opening them again and continuing. I watched her fight the urge to fall asleep while she sucked the last drops out of the bottle, then dozed off again on my arm. I then put her down in her crib and watched her for a few seconds until she was completely out. I snuck out of the room, then walked downstairs, my mind still circling the events in Washington. There was the matter of the missing surveillance footage and the fact that Yossi David knew where to find Kimmie at the safe house. Could the FBI have a leak? And now it was like Isabella didn't even want to get my statement? What was that all about?

I grabbed a cup, poured coffee in it from the pot, and then stared out at the canal behind my house. A flock of pelicans flew by, floating through the air, then dove into the water with a huge splash, trying to get the fish below.

Watching this spectacular show, as they dove in one after the other, I couldn't stop thinking about Samantha Durkin, who was murdered. I knew absolutely nothing about her. Had Wanton really killed her simply because she didn't want to sleep with him and Kimmie? It seemed a little excessive, I thought. It had to be more than that. Had she maybe threatened to expose him? To go to the media?

But why would he murder her himself and risk getting seen and caught when he apparently easily could hire an assassin as we saw with Kimmie? Why not just let her go and then send someone after her?

Why would a man as powerful as Richard Wanton risk everything by murdering her? You'd assume he was smarter than that.

Right?

Chapter 35

THEN:

SHE HAD DECIDED to stay strong, to resist him the next time he tried something. A month later, after Samantha had met with Wanton in the restroom, she still felt so dirty that she could barely focus on her work. She felt like everyone knew what had happened and looked at her differently, talking about her behind her back, laughing at her for sleeping her way to the top. She couldn't blame them for thinking that way. She knew how it looked.

And now, she had decided to end it.

Samantha did want to climb high in the ranks, and her dream was to be an anchor one day. But not this way. She didn't want to look back at her career and know that it was because she had slept with Wanton.

She didn't want it this way.

And she couldn't do it anymore. After what happened in the restroom, she could barely look at her own reflection in the mirror;

that's how disgusted she was with herself. She dreamed about it at night, waking up bathed in sweat, scared anyone would know. During the day at the TV station, she was so afraid that people could somehow see it on her—that they knew what she had let him do to her.

Samantha shivered at the thought while sitting by her computer screen, writing the manuscript for a story she was doing. She had been working like crazy ever since it happened, trying to prove to herself and others that she was worthy of her internship, that she was a good reporter. Her friend Natasha complained that she never got to see her anymore, that she was never home, and that she was working herself too hard, but it was all she knew how to do right now. She wanted to become a reporter, a good one. And working was the only thing that made her forget what she had done. But once she closed her eyes, it was there again and again. Him grabbing her by the hips and turning her around. The way he pushed her down over the toilet. She could still feel his hands on her and hear his groans behind her.

It haunted her.

You gotta let it go. You gotta stop thinking about it. Focus on your work.

But the disgust was hard to get rid of. Words like whore and slut circled in her mind constantly, and as the days passed, she felt worse and worse about herself. When the other interns went out for a drink, she didn't go with them. When the colleagues went for a bite to eat after a broadcast, she didn't go, and she stayed in the newsroom, covering herself with work.

She could barely recognize herself. Natasha had begun to say things too. Like she was getting boring—like the job had become her boyfriend, and as early as the day before, she had asked her if it was something Natasha had done. If she was angry with her?

"It's not. I swear," Sam had said.

"Then, what is wrong? You used to be so much fun? We used to go out all the time. You're the party girl, remember? You're the one who dances on the bar counter, so all the guys look at you, wishing they were with you, and all the girls stare, wishing they were you, that they had your confidence. I'm the boring one, and you're the one who drags me out of my comfort zone. What if we go out tonight? Maybe we'll meet those cute guys again like last time? Remember how you told me to put myself out there more?"

"I...I don't...I'm not sure I think you should anymore; nothing good can come from that," Samantha had said, then added: "I'm busy. I'll call you later."

She had hung up on her before she could protest. There was no way Samantha could explain to Natasha what was going on with her because she wasn't sure she understood it herself.

She stared at her screen, barely blinking, when a message ticked in in the corner. Samantha stared at it, not knowing what to do.

Then, she opened it.

WE'RE GOING FOR A RIDE IN MY CAR. COME OUT BACK AND MEET ME THERE. NOW.

Samantha stopped breathing. She looked at the words from Wanton, her heart sinking. It had been a month. She truly believed he had grown tired of her by now, that he'd leave her alone. She bit the side of her cheek, wondering what to say, how to respond. There was no way she was going anywhere with him in his car; that was for sure. Not after what had happened last time in the bathroom—not after he had made it perfectly clear what kind of relationship he wanted with her.

I'm going to have some fun with you.

That's how he had put it. And he had had his fun. But it wasn't going any further than that. It was going to end here.

She leaned over the keyboard and started to type:

I CAN'T.

Then she pressed enter to send it, feeling strong, telling herself it was the right thing to do.

The answer didn't wait long to come.

YOU HAVE TO. MEET ME NOW.

Samantha shook her head at this. Even if she had wanted to, she really couldn't since she was going into the editing suite in just fifteen minutes.

I CAN'T. I AM WORKING. I HAVE TO EDIT MY STORY SOON. I CAN'T LEAVE. MY PRODUCER WILL KILL ME.

Trying to stand firm, forcing herself to follow through with this, she leaned back in her office chair, heart throbbing in her chest, waiting for his reply.

It came fast.

YOU HAVE TO. COME NOW.

Samantha wrinkled her forehead. Was this guy for real? Wasn't he the head of the entire network? Didn't he understand that work came first? That the story had to come first? Didn't he want her to do her job?

I CAN'T, she wrote, feeling stubborn and annoyed with him now.

A pause followed before the next message arrived:

COME. NOW.

She couldn't believe him; why didn't he give up? She wrote again:

I REALLY CAN'T. I'LL GET FIRED.

She knew that Wanton could probably stop that from happening, but she didn't know if he would do that for her or if he'd just toss her in the street, not caring while moving on to the next girl. She wasn't stupid enough to believe he actually cared for her.

YOU MUST COME NOW!

She was staring at the screen when her producer came to her desk, and she closed the window quickly without answering, so he wouldn't see who she was messaging.

"Why aren't you in editing?"

She rose to her feet, laptop in her hands. "I'm going now."

"Better get a move on!" he yelled after her as she rushed out of the newsroom and down the hall. She found the editing suite and sat down with a guy they called The Bear because of his size and similarity to one.

He smiled at her, and she smiled back.

"So, what are we doing today?" he asked.

She explained her story to him, and as he found the footage on his computer, she opened her laptop and logged onto the system again, terrified of seeing more messages from Wanton.

There was one. She opened it, heart beating fast in her chest. It said:

JUST MESSING WITH YOU. SEE YOU LATER.

Chapter 36

John was sitting in his office when he saw his wife stroll past the glass windows and storm inside. He got up from his chair, startled.

"Carol? What are you doing here?"

She smiled. "Just checking in. I was close by and wondered if you'd like to grab lunch with me."

He looked at his watch. "I have a meeting in ten minutes that I can't miss."

She tilted her head. "Ah, that's too bad." She looked around, then sat down in a chair. John felt uneasy.

"I saw the new intern sitting in the newsroom. She's pretty."

John sighed and sat on the edge of his desk. "I told you, Carol. There are no others. I am being a good boy."

She smiled. It came off sarcastically. "That's right. You told me that."

"Is there anything else you need right now? Because I have to get to the meeting. Wanton will be there, and he's pissed."

She nodded. "I bet he is."

"So...can I do something for you now? Because otherwise, I need to get back to preparing for this meeting."

"Of course, of course," she said.

Yet, she didn't make any attempt at getting up or walking out. John watched her, puzzled.

"What's going on?"

"I was just thinking..."

"About what?"

"The girl that was killed."

John sighed. "Samantha. She jumped. Wanton told us the truth, remember? She was crazy; she was screaming at him, and then she jumped to her death. It wasn't Wanton's fault. I know you think it was, but he's our friend and my boss, and we have to believe him."

She nodded. "Yes, yes, of course, we must. He's done so much for you, for us, really. Creating this great career for you, making you who you are."

"Exactly. I have known him for twenty-five years, Carol. He might be a pig, but he's no murderer."

Carol nodded again. "Of course. Silly me."

She rose to her feet and seemed like she was about to leave when she paused. She turned her head and looked at him.

"Did you know her?"

"Did I know who?"

"The girl who allegedly jumped to her death? I mean, she worked here, right?"

John's eyes grew wide; then, he shook his head. "Her name was Samantha. I knew who she was, yes, but I didn't know her personally."

Carol nodded pensively. "Did you sleep with her?"

John wrinkled his forehead.

"Why on earth would you ask me about that?"

Carol looked down at her fingers, then shook her head.

"Just wondering."

He rubbed his forehead. "Carol, what happened, happened once.

I did as you told me to and had her transferred to another department with Richard's help. It's over; I told you this. Now, will you please just let me get ready for this meeting?"

She nodded while smiling, then leaned over and kissed him on the cheek.

"Of course. See you tonight."

Chapter 37

"Any more mashed potatoes?"

I looked at my kids around the table. Alex was staring into his plate and had barely eaten anything, maybe because I had yelled at him for getting in trouble at school again. They were threatening to suspend him, and I had to go talk to the principal tomorrow and try to convince her to let him stay. His behavior had improved ever since he was enrolled in the gifted program, and he got more challenges, but he still had trouble remaining calm in the classroom. He got bored so easily, and that's when he usually got himself in trouble. I was getting frustrated with him because he knew better.

"You're too smart for this," I had told him.

Now, he was mad at me and refusing to eat his dinner. I tried not to pay any attention to him.

"Christine?"

I held up the bowl of mashed potatoes. She shook her head.

"Olivia? You want more?"

Olivia didn't react. She sat looking down, and I tilted my head.

"Olivia?"

"She's on her phone," Christine said in a whiny tone.

"No phones at the table," Alex yelled. "You know the rules!"

Olivia lifted her glare and met Christine's. "You couldn't just leave it alone, could you?"

"Why should you be allowed on your phone if I'm not?" Christine said.

"You're such a..."

"Olivia!" I cut through. "I'm gonna stop you right there before you say something I don't approve of and get yourself grounded. Christine is right. You know the rules."

She sighed and put the phone down. I smiled and finished my food. "What's so important anyway that it can't wait?"

"Nothing," Olivia said and shook her head. "Can I be excused?"

I narrowed my eyes. Something was going on with her. I nodded and let her get up. The other kids followed immediately after like they couldn't get away from me fast enough. I cleaned up the kitchen while Angel sat in her pen, holding a small cup I had given her like it was the Holy Grail.

I was putting the dishes in the washer when Olivia came back down.

"Hi, sweetie." I gave her a curious look. "What's going on?"

She shook her head, then approached me and started to help me put silverware in the washer. I sensed she wanted to talk but let her get ready on her own.

"Say..."

I stopped, a plate still clutched in my hand. "Yes?"

"I thought you said that Tristan was staying with his grandmother? Doesn't she live in Texas or something?"

I nodded. "Yes, that's what I've been told. Why?"

She looked pensive. "Hm."

I wrinkled my nose. "Why do you ask?"

She shook her head. "No, it's just that...well, he...maybe it's nothing."

"No, Olivia, it's not nothing. Or you wouldn't be here asking me about it."

She exhaled. "It's just that someone tagged him in a photo on Instagram just a few hours ago. And he is definitely not in Texas since it's snowing where he is. I know it snows in Texas but not at this time of year."

I shrugged. "Maybe the grandmother took him skiing?"

"Maybe. But he's with some girl."

"He could have met her at the place they're staying," I said.

"They're not on a slope; they're sitting in a yard," she said. "There doesn't seem to be mountains around them, look."

She showed me the picture, and I took the phone from between her hands, then studied it closer. It didn't look at all like a skiing area. It was snowing, yes, but just a light dusting was on the ground. It wasn't cold enough for it to stay, which meant it wasn't a skiing area.

"Maybe they're visiting some people they know," I said.

She shrugged again. "Yeah, you're probably right. I'm just worried about him, you know?"

"I can't blame you."

Olivia left, and I finished cleaning up. I then sat down at my laptop and opened Facebook. I went to Kimmie's page, where hundreds of people had written their condolences to her family and wrote how much they would miss her and how wonderful a person she was. I then found her mother's profile and clicked it. There she was, Kimmie's mother, who was from Texas, just as Olivia had said. Kimmie's mother had many pictures of herself on her profile and photos of her with a man she seemed very fond of, but who clearly wasn't Kimmie's father as he was very dark. Kimmie's mother, who had recently moved, according to her updates.

Kimmie's mother, who now lived in...Morocco?

Chapter 38

I stared at the screen for a long time, my fingers tapping on the table while thinking this through, going through all the possible explanations. But each and every one came to the same conclusion.

I picked up my phone and called Isabella.

"You lied to me."

"Excuse me?" she said.

"You told me that Tristan would go live with his grandmother."

She paused. "And?"

"And he's very obviously not living with her since she's in Morocco, of all places. I know he only has one grandmother since he doesn't know who his father is. No matter how I turn this and look at it from different sides, I can only conclude that you lied to me. My question is, why? You know I worry about the kid. He's my daughter's friend."

Isabella cleared her throat. "I'm afraid I can't discuss this with you. You're not on the case anymore, and this is confidential information."

"Ah, don't give me that," I groaned.

She exhaled. "You know I can't say anything else."

"At least tell me he's with family."

"Okay, he's with family. I can tell you that much." She went quiet, then continued. "Was there anything else, Eva Rae? I'm busy here."

I paused. "It's just that...he doesn't really have much family. All Kimmie had was her mother. She had no siblings. So, who is he with then? Is he all right being with them? Because he's always welcome here..."

Isabella interrupted me with a deep groan. "Eva Rae Thomas! Tristan is fine. Trust me. He's with a close relative."

"Where? Where is he? Is he safe? Do these people know how to protect him? Do they care for him?"

"God, you're annoying. Yes, they've got it under control. We sent him to Texas with some relatives. There, you have it. It's all I can say. Now, please, leave it alone, okay? I know you feel guilty and responsible for the boy, and that's very honorable of you. You have a big heart. And we're grateful for all your help with Kimmie and the case, but let us take it from here."

"But...I'm just not..."

"Bye, Eva Rae."

Then, she hung up. I stared at the phone's display, my pulse quickening. Isabella was acting very strange about this, and I didn't like it.

And what was worse, she had just lied to me again.

If there was one thing I had learned, it was that Tristan wasn't in Texas. He was nowhere near the South.

The question was, where was he then, and who was he with? Was he really with family, as Isabella said? Why would she continue to lie to me?

What was Isabella hiding?

Chapter 39

"It's really hard for me to talk about, so I wrote it all down."

Rachel sat with the papers between her hands, two pages she had written on the computer in the dead of night while everyone else in the house was asleep. She had been lying awake, thinking about what Crystal had told her the day before at the restaurant. How Rachel wasn't the only one it had happened to, that she had a handful of other girls who had already told her their stories, and they were collecting them to start a case against Wanton.

A sexual harassment case.

Just hearing the words leave Crystal's lips had made Rachel's hands begin to shake. She was terrified of having another panic attack and had to excuse herself and go to the bathroom to splash water on her face to cool herself down. It felt like she was going to burn up.

Later, at home, while lying in bed, she couldn't sleep. It felt like someone had ripped her mind open. She had this picture in her mind of a dam, keeping the water in, and now, there was a crack in it. Water had started to pour out, but soon the crack would open wider, and the water would start flooding out. Once that happened, there was no way back, and the flood would take over.

That's how it felt.

Rachel knew that she had opened up for this. Seeing Wanton on TV had somehow ripped something open inside her, and now it was beginning to leak. She wondered if she would be able to stop the flood from happening. Would she be able to put it all back in her mind and close the lid again? Or was it too late? Would she survive it if she let the crack get deeper? If she let out more?

She had closed her eyes, trying to force sleep to come, but it didn't. On the contrary, she felt more awake than ever, and now these images were beginning to flash by. She saw him, and she saw his hand on top of her mouth. She felt the powerlessness as he put his weight into it, and she was pushed down.

Then she gasped for air and opened her eyes.

I can't do this. I can't do this. I can't think about it. I just can't.

But the images wouldn't go away; they kept coming at her like the flood from the dam, getting more and more violent, the bigger the crack got, and soon, she had to get out of bed in order to sustain it. She was gasping for air, holding her throat as she staggered into the kitchen, then into her office, and sat down at the computer. She had stared at the dark screen for a long time, trying hard simply to breathe and make sense of things.

Then she had begun to write. She had no idea what she was writing but just let it flow—word for word onto the paper, telling the story of what had happened, saying the words she had never dared to utter to anyone else, not even her loved ones.

Now, she was handing the pieces of paper to Crystal, who had come to her house after Rachel had called her and told her she was ready to talk.

Crystal stared at the papers, then up at Rachel.

"This is my story. It is something I have never told anyone, so please keep it to yourself for now." Rachel took in a deep breath before continuing:

"But as you will see when reading it...I...I was raped by Richard Wanton."

Chapter 40

I couldn't sleep. Angel woke up every hour and wanted her bottle, so I sat with her most of the night while staring out the window, a million thoughts rushing through my mind. When I wasn't staring out the window, I was on my phone, scrolling through Tristan's Instagram account, looking especially long at the picture that Olivia had shown me. The one where he was with the girl in the snow. Her name was Haley. The caption read:

Hanging in the snow with my new friend.

"Texas, pfft," I snorted. "This is April. They had seventy-seven degrees in Houston today."

Even the trees in the background were too bare to belong to that part of the country. There was no way it was taken in Texas. I then Googled a few things and found out where it had been snowing around the date that the picture was posted. There had been a cold front moving through the east coast, dropping snow from Washington to Boston. That's where he had to be—not down south, as Isabella said.

Liar!

"But where are you, Tristan, and who are you with then?" I

mumbled like a madman at my phone while Angel fell back to sleep in her crib. I felt so angry with Isabella. I could tolerate many things but not being lied to.

Why did she feel the need to lie to me?

I tried to go back to bed but couldn't sleep. How could I? All I worried about was the boy, Tristan. I sat back up, grabbed my phone again, then did something I knew I would regret later on, yet did it anyway.

I asked to follow Haley and waited for her to accept. Even though it was late, she did, and I wrote a private message to her, asking her about Tristan. I told her I was an old friend, and I was worried about him since he had been through a lot. I just wanted to know that he was okay and that he was with people who cared for him.

Feeling good about my decision, I put the phone down, then went to sleep, finally dozing off. When I woke up the following day, I had received a message from her, and I opened it.

Hello, Mrs. Thomas. I am sad to say that I don't think Tristan is doing very well. He just moved in next door, so I don't know much about his situation. But something isn't right if you ask me. It seems like they're keeping him like a prisoner inside of their house, and he has to sneak out to see me. He's not even allowed to go outside, but he does it anyway, crawling out the window in the back. He seems really sad and won't talk to me about his past or why he's staying in that house and not allowed to leave. He's not even allowed to have a phone, and he doesn't go to school. It's sad because I really like him. I'll tell him you wrote to me when I meet him tonight.

I stared at the words on my screen, barely blinking. They were keeping him like a prisoner? Not allowing him to have a phone? What the heck was this? Who were these people? Family? Why were they doing this to him? Hadn't he been through enough?

I wrote her back:

Thank you for letting me know this. Please, don't tell him anything. I will come for a surprise visit and talk to him myself. Could you tell me where you live?

I sat back while waiting for the response. It came right away.

I am sorry. I can't do that. You'll have to excuse me, but I don't know you very well. I'm sorry.

I grumbled, annoyed at this. Of course, teenagers today were so careful, growing up in the age of social media.

But I wasn't giving up just yet. Instead, I scrolled through Haley's profile until I found a picture of her in front of what I assumed had to be her school. Then I Googled the school's name, which, to my luck, wasn't a common one, and it turned up with the full address. I plotted it down and got it pinned on a map, then realized it was located in a small town north of Baltimore. I nodded, thinking it wasn't uncommon for small flurries of snowflakes to fall there in the month of April, even though they would melt quickly.

"Thank you, Haley," I said, then went online to book a ticket to Baltimore.

Chapter 41

THEN:

"It's been forever. How are you doing?"

Natasha placed a pot of herbal tea in front of Samantha. They were sitting in the kitchen of Nat's one-bedroom apartment. It had been so long since Samantha had been there; she had forgotten how small the place was. Nat was a terrible messy head, and there were stacks of books on the table, along with clothing on the backs of all the chairs. A wet towel was on the floor, and Natasha saw Samantha look at it, then picked it up. Natasha found some cookies, put them in front of her, and then sat down by the small wooden table, pushing away a book.

Natasha had just started working for a publishing house and hoped to become an editor one day. Her heart belonged in books, even though she couldn't write one if her life depended on it. She knew what could be done to make them better.

"I'm great," Samantha said.

"What have you been up to?" Natasha asked as she sat down and poured them both some tea. "And don't say *just working* because I don't buy that. No one works that much. There must be something else involved. A guy, maybe? Did you meet someone?" she paused and scrutinized Samantha's face, then nodded.

"That's what I thought."

Sam shook her head. "No, no. It's not what you think at all. I've just been really into the work. I want to get good at it and get interesting stories, you know? But that requires a lot of me, like me being there all the time. If you want a big career in journalism, you have to go all in."

Natasha nodded and blew on her cup. "I guess I can understand that. It just worries me a little, you know? All work and no play and all that."

Samantha laughed. It didn't sound sincere, and she got lost for a second in her own thoughts while sipping her cup. Natasha always had the best teas. She'd go to these small Asian shops and buy them. She could spend hours talking to the owners about something as simple as tea, which was basically just a bunch of leaves. Sam had always admired her friend's ability to get a lot out of almost nothing. Natasha enjoyed life. And when she found something she liked, she'd go all in till she knew everything there was to know about it, not leaving one little detail to go undiscovered.

"You're sure you're okay?" Natasha asked.

Samantha sipped her cup, then nodded. "Yes. I'm really great, as a matter of fact."

She added a smile that soon became stiff, and she looked into the liquid in the cup between her hands.

"Do you want to order Thai food tonight like we used to?" Nat asked, lifting a couple of books from the table, looking for the menu from their favorite place. She found it and pulled it out from beneath a stack of books.

"I could really go for some pad Thai; how about you?"

Samantha hadn't been listening and looked up. "What's that?"

"Here. Pick yours," she said and handed her the menu. "I know what I want."

Sam looked at the menu. "Oh, yeah, of course."

She stared at the meals, unable to choose when her phone started to vibrate on the table in front of her. Nat looked at it, and Sam grabbed it before she could see the display. Sam stared at it, her heart sinking.

It was him.

Chapter 42

I sighed, exhausted at the lady behind the counter at the AVIS rental car place. She had just told me she wanted more money from me—some sort of extra insurance because of the weather.

"The roads are slippery due to the snowfall we just had. It's a little crazy with snow in April. It's like spring won't come this year."

I shook my head. This was getting to be a costly case for me with all the flying back and forth. I was alone now in paying my mortgage, and Matt hadn't paid alimony for Angel yet. And with all these last-minute tickets flying up north, I was soon running out of money.

"I'll take my chances," I said and took the car keys.

"Okay. Just know it'll be expensive in case something happens to the car."

I nodded, annoyed, then left and ran to my car. I threw my bag in the back, then got in and found my phone, where I had plotted in the address for the school. It was located in a town twenty-seven miles west of Baltimore, almost thirty miles from the airport. It wouldn't take me long to get there. It was early in the afternoon, so I had time to get there and start looking for Tristan before it got dark. I checked my phone and messages one last time before taking off from the airport parking lot—nothing from my mom, who was taking care of all the kids, even Angel. I was a little nervous about that part, but she had done it before, and Olivia was there to help her if she needed it. Olivia could easily get up with Angel at night. She was really good at taking care of her.

It's gonna be okay.

I drove onto the highway, sped up the car, and reached the town by two o'clock. I stopped at a gas station and grabbed a sandwich and a soda along with some coffee before driving past the city limit sign:

Sykesville. Population 4,197. Named 'Coolest Small Town in America' by BudgetTravel.com in 2016.

I drove straight into the historic district with the beautiful old buildings from the late-eighteen-hundreds. Sykesville was one of the first railroad lines in the US, and the B&O train station one of the oldest buildings there. The town's main street was cute enough to have been taken out of a movie. Signs telling me the farmer's market would return later this spring welcomed me from the lampposts.

I continued not much farther until I reached the yellow brick building that I recognized from the photo on Haley's Instagram page. I stopped the car in front of it, then looked at the sign over the entrance, where I had seen Haley standing with her friends from the lacrosse team, wearing their uniforms, cheering after winning their very first game last year.

I shut off the engine and looked at my watch. Now, all I had to do was wait. Feeling like an actual stalker, I sat by the entrance to the school and waited until the bell rang, and all the kids began rushing out. I stared at each and every face until finally, I saw the one I recognized—the girl from the photo with Tristan.

I watched her walk to her car and get in. Then I started my engine and followed her.

Chapter 43

"Do you have any evidence, any witnesses that can confirm your story?"

Crystal had read what Rachel had written down, or rather poured from her bleeding heart, she would rather call it.

Crystal's eyes were lingering on Rachel.

"I...no, I don't. And no one who would testify on my behalf, no."

Crystal exhaled. She looked briefly at the paper, then shook her head. "I... I am so sorry this happened to you. I truly am."

Crystal had tears in her eyes as she looked at Rachel, and now Rachel was tearing up as well.

"And you were alone with him in the apartment?"

"Well, not at first since, as I wrote, a colleague told me that they were all going to his apartment and that it was like a party. But then when I got there, it was only the two of them. And that's when I realized this was planned. They knew I would never have gone up there if I thought I'd be alone with them or with Wanton. I believed there were going to be a lot of people. That's what he told me, the guy who brought me there. That everyone was going."

"And then it was just those two, huh. That's when they told you?"

Rachel swallowed hard, then looked down at her fingers. Talking about this, saying it out loud was so much harder than writing everything down. When saying it out loud, it became so real.

"One of them blocked the door, and then Wanton asked me if I had ever had a threesome," she said with a sniffle. "I told them I hadn't, and then they asked if I wanted to try it. I said no, and panic began to erupt inside me since I couldn't get to the door where this other guy was standing. I told them I wasn't interested, then began walking away. Wanton then asked me if I was serious about my career as a reporter, and I said that I was, but I didn't want it this way."

Rachel stopped talking to catch her breath. Her throat was getting so narrow—it was like it was closing up the more of her story she let out of it. Like it was trying to stop the words from flowing.

She drank water to calm herself, praying she didn't have another anxiety attack. Her flushing cheeks were a warning sign.

Please. Not now. Please.

The more she thought about it, the more her heart began to race, and the sound of her rapid pulse was pounding in her ears.

"What did they do?'

Rachel focused on Crystal, trying to swallow the knot growing in her throat, pressing back the desire to scream, cry, and run. This was it. If she were ever to tell her story, if she was ever to get back at Wanton for what he did, then it was now. Either she spoke now, or she held her silence forever.

Don't let him get away with it.

"I'm sorry," she said and wiped away a tear. "It's just...well... humiliating. I have been so angry at myself for what happened for many years..."

Crystal reached out her hand and put it on top of Rachel's. "Remember who you're talking to. I have my own story, too, okay?

You're not alone. What happened wasn't your fault. Do you hear me?"

Rachel nodded. "Okay."

"Tell me what happened next; take your time."

"Then they...Wanton he...came closer and closer, and he grabbed me and started to...undress me. I cried and told him I didn't want to." Rachel trailed off, her heart bouncing so hard it hurt her chest. She gasped for air, and no more words left her lips for several minutes until she finally composed herself.

"I just gave in," she said. "I didn't scream; I didn't kick or hit. I just...gave up. And I hate myself for that. I kept blaming myself, telling myself it was my own fault all these years because I went there willingly—because I didn't put up a fight. I'm not that kind of girl. You must understand. I don't do things like that. Yet I couldn't seem to stop it from happening, and now I can't stop wondering if I put this on myself somehow. If I made him believe that I was into something like that—if I somehow led him on? I have been feeling so shameful about this that I never told anyone."

Crystal nodded, tears springing to her eyes. "He was your boss. He is the one to blame. He's the one who is responsible. I'm so sorry, sweetie. But as I told you, you're not alone. If only you knew how many girls I have talked to who can tell pretty much the same story. We'll get him. Together, all of us will take him down for what he has done."

Chapter 44

Haley stopped her old Toyota Camry in front of a small farmhouse outside of town. I watched her park on the long newly-paved driveway, then walk up to the porch and enter. I then parked across the street from her and sat there for a few minutes, scanning the area. We were out in the country now, and the houses were far apart, with lots of land surrounding them. I looked at the neighboring houses, wondering if Tristan was inside any of them.

How did he end up out here? Was he with relatives? Maybe some distant cousin? And why on earth was Isabella so secretive about it?

I sat there for about fifteen minutes until I spotted Haley leaving her house again on foot. She walked across the driveway and into the yard next door, then disappeared behind the small house.

"Where are you going?" I mumbled, then got out of the car. I walked up to the neighboring house and snuck up its side until I reached the corner. I peeked around it, then held my breath.

It was Haley. She was sitting on the back porch with someone —a boy.

Tristan.

I pulled back, so they wouldn't see me, then stood there for a few minutes, listening to them talk. I was thrilled to have found him and could hardly believe it, but at the same time, I had no idea exactly what to do next. Could I approach him? I hadn't thought this through, I realized. I just wanted to make sure he was okay and not in any danger. As he sat there with the girl, he seemed fine. But who was he living with? Who were these people who wouldn't let him go to school or go outside, or even have a phone? I had to make sure he was okay.

I wasn't leaving until I knew.

I started to wonder how to talk to him, to get him alone so he could speak freely, then thought, *now is as good a time as ever*. I was about to turn around the corner and just face him, ask him if he was okay or if he needed my help when I heard another voice come from inside and pulled back again. I held my breath while listening. Someone had come out to them. The voice was telling Tristan to come back inside.

"You know they don't want you out here, Tristan," it said. "It's too dangerous. And don't let them see you with her either. You'll get us all in trouble."

"But..." Tristan complained. "Haley is my friend. She's the only one keeping me from going insane out here. I have no phone, no social life; all we have is that damn old TV in there to keep me entertained."

"I know it's a lot to ask of you," the voice continued. "But for now, it has to be this way. You can see Haley all you want once this is over."

I stared down at my hands. They were shaking as I listened to this woman's voice. I couldn't believe my own ears. I knew this voice. I knew this voice very well. But it couldn't be. I had to be wrong.

I took in a deep breath, then peeked around the corner once again to see who she was with my own eyes. As I laid my eyes on her, my heart stopped.

What the heck was going on?

Chapter 45

THEN:

"Who's 'W?'"

Natasha looked at Samantha's display just as she picked the phone up from the table. Their eyes met, and Nat could immediately sense something was off. Samantha had saved his number under W for Wanton. Just in case anyone peeked through her contacts or—like now—he called when she was with someone.

"I...I have to take this," Sam said as she got up and walked into the living room of Nat's apartment, phone clutched tightly to her ear, hoping that her friend couldn't hear her speak.

"H-hello?"

The voice on the other end was cheerful. "Hello, Samantha?"

She slightly trembled when hearing his voice. "Y-yes?"

"It's the big bad CEO."

Samantha stood with the phone pressed against her ear, staring at a window in front of her. A bird was pecking at something on the small balcony. She didn't know what to respond.

"Hi," she simply said, trying to sound like she wasn't about to cry. What did he want? Why was he calling her on her cell?

"What are you doing? Are you sitting all alone in your small apartment?"

"N-no."

"I was thinking about stopping by."

"But I'm not...I am at a friend's place across town."

Silence. She could hear Wanton breathing on the other end. "Really? Because I could come by."

Samantha narrowed her eyes. Wasn't he hearing her? Was he expecting her simply to sit and wait for him? Or to throw everything she had in her hands to be ready for him to stop by?

"I'm not...I can't."

Another silence.

"Where are you? I can pick you up."

Samantha heard steps coming up behind her and saw Nat approaching. Her eyes were worried. Sam signaled for her to be quiet as she looked like she was about to speak.

"I can't do that. I'm sorry."

"Oh, you're sorry, are you?" he sounded agitated now. She could hear he was smoking a cigarette and knew exactly how aggressively he was blowing out smoke.

Her eyes met Nat's. "Yes, I'm...I can't do this. I'm visiting a friend."

"Really? I think you should come back *now*."

The way he said now made Sam jump. In the beginning, she had been flattered by his attention, the stolen glances, the warm smiles, but now?

It was beginning to take a turn she wasn't comfortable with.

"Listen, I told you I'm at a friend's place, and I can't just..."

Click.

The line went dead.

"Hello?"

Samantha stared at the phone, her cheeks blushing. Nat approached her, her head slightly tilted, a deep furrow growing between her eyebrows.

"Who was that?"

Samantha took in a deep breath to calm herself. Her hand holding the phone was trembling. She pressed back tears and looked at her friend.

"It was no one. Just some work. They wanted me to come in, but..."

Nat placed a hand on her arm. "Are you in some kind of trouble?"

Samantha sniffled, then shook her head. "No. Not at all. I got it under control."

"Are you sure? Look at me, Sam. You can tell me if you're in trouble."

She lifted her gaze and looked into her friend's eyes, then nodded. "I'm positive. It's nothing."

Chapter 46

"Stop sulking."

Kimmie groaned and rolled her eyes at her son. Tristan grumbled something and followed her back inside while the girl living next door, Haley, left. Kimmie saw how her son looked after her as she walked across the lawn back to her home, and she felt awful. It was the first time she had seen her son in love, and he wasn't even able to be with her. It broke her heart.

Kimmie hated herself for putting him in this situation.

"It's for our own good; you know this."

She closed the door behind him, and they went back inside where the two FBI agents were sitting by the door. The big guy to the left was the one who had told her to get her son back inside. He risked being seen. Kimmie had asked him who the heck would see Tristan all the way out in the boonies and recognize him? But there was no way to make them bend the rules.

"I know. I know," Tristan said and threw himself on the old brown leather couch with a deep sigh. "They tried to kill us, and if they know you're still alive, they might try again. I know. It's just...so..."

She sat next to him, wincing in pain as she did. The wound in her chest where she was shot still hurt, and she became easily very tired during the day.

Kimmie placed a hand on his knee. "I know, sweetie. This isn't my choice either. You know this."

Tristan looked at her. "I know you're doing something big and important, Mom. And I am proud of you for standing up to someone like Wanton and testifying against him. I really am. I just wish that it would be over soon, so we could have a life again."

Kimmie felt herself tear up. It was the first time Tristan had acknowledged what she was doing and told her he was proud of her. That was a big deal for her.

"I know, son, and we will. But we must be patient." She paused to swallow the knot in her throat. She had felt so guilty for so long about what she was doing; it had been painful. She hated that she had destroyed Tristan's life by doing this. She loathed the fact that he was hurt. Hearing him say those words hit her hard.

"So...that girl...you really like her, huh?"

He shrugged. "I guess. She's okay."

Kimmie chuckled. "I've seen you with her. And I've seen the way she looks at you. A mother notices little things like that."

He smiled, then rolled his eyes. "Mo-om, you're so cringy right now. You have no idea; I can't even..."

She shrugged. "Well, I'm a mother. I'm supposed to be."

Kimmie smiled and looked at her handsome son. She had noticed him sneaking out late at night, crawling out the bedroom window, and knew he went to see Haley but pretended like she didn't know the next morning. She wanted him to have a life, at least as much as possible with their situation. And she really didn't see any harm in him meeting with this girl out in the country. It wasn't like anyone would know who he was out here. Besides, it was Kimmie they were looking for, and if she stayed inside, then she'd be good. Plus, they all thought she was dead. The FBI had arranged it this way to keep her safe.

Who would go looking for a dead woman anyway?

Chapter 47

"She's alive? Kimmie's alive?"

I was almost screaming the words inside my rental car. I had run back to it and got in, barely breathing after seeing her.

Isabella had lied to me? She had told me Kimmie died? She had let me believe that Kimmie died on my watch, that I had failed her!

"I'm gonna kill her," I screamed out in the car. I grabbed for my phone in my pocket, then found her number and pressed call.

No answer.

I tried again, but still, she didn't pick up.

"Because you don't want to talk to me," I yelled at the phone, "I wouldn't talk to me either if I were you. But you can't avoid me forever, and then I'll tell you what I think about you. Boy, am I gonna let you know."

I threw the phone on the passenger seat with an annoyed groan. I slammed my hands into the steering wheel over and over again, imagining it was Isabella. I couldn't believe she'd do this to me. She knew how much I suffered. She knew how badly I took Kimmie's death.

And she'd been alive all this time?

"Oh, I am gonna kill you, Isabella. I'm gonna..."

I grabbed my soda and drank from it, but it had gone flat, so it tasted awful. I put it back down, checked my phone again, texted Isabella to call me asap, and put it away. I closed my eyes, rubbed them, annoyed, then wondered what to do next.

There really wasn't anything more for me to do here, was there? I had found out who Tristan was with. I knew he was with his mother, protected by the FBI. They had probably decided to fake her death so Wanton's people wouldn't look for her anymore, to protect both of them. It was a smart enough move, one I would have made too had it been up to me.

Except I would have told myself the truth and not lied. It puzzled me that Isabella didn't think she could trust me enough to tell me. It didn't make much sense to me right at this moment.

We had known each other for years. She knew me better than most. Plus, she trusted me enough to pull me in to help on the case when Kimmie asked for me. They wanted me to interview Kimmie. Why didn't they want me to know she was alive?

It didn't make sense to me. And I didn't like it. Something wasn't right about this, even though I couldn't put my finger on precisely what it was that mystified me.

I started the car back up, thinking if I got back to the airport, I could maybe catch a late flight out and be home by midnight with a little luck. Or perhaps I could find a small hotel, stay there the night, and then fly out in the morning. I let the car roll down the street, then turned right at the intersection and drove onto a wider road when a silver-gray car passed me on the way, and for some reason, I got a glimpse of the driver.

He didn't see me, but I most certainly saw him.

And his red New York Yankees baseball cap.

Chapter 48

It can't be!

I stared at the silver-gray car in the rearview mirror as it disappeared down the road. My heart was throbbing violently in my chest as I watched it take the turn, driving back where I had just come from. I could barely breathe.

Was that really Yossi I had seen?

I wasn't sure.

I slowed my rental car down and let it come to a stop while a million thoughts rushed through my mind.

Then, I made a U-turn and drove back, stepping on the accelerator. My tires screeched on the asphalt as I took the turn up the narrow street back toward the farmhouse. In the distance, I could see that the silver-gray car had stopped right in front of it, in front of the house where I had seen Kimmie and Tristan. And the person with the red cap got out and rushed up toward the porch.

Oh, dear Lord, no!

I raced up the narrow road while watching Yossi stride toward the stairs. He then pulled a gun and shot one of the guards who had come out and was sitting by the door, quickly and without even wincing.

The way only an assassin could.

I jumped in my seat, my heart bouncing in my throat. I was too late, wasn't I? Just because I hadn't been certain when I saw him, just because I had to stop and think before I drove back, I had killed them all. Why couldn't I just have reacted faster? Why couldn't I have trusted my instinct?

Yossi kicked the door open and fired another shot. I screamed inside my car when seeing it, then closed my eyes in fear as more shots fell.

Please! No!

Tears streamed across my cheeks as the realization sank in, and I once again opened my eyes to look. As I did, my eyes fell on something moving behind the farmhouse, two bodies rushing across the empty field next to it, huddling together.

Tristan and Kimmie!

I could barely believe my eyes. They had to have somehow snuck out the back of the house when Yossi entered and started shooting. I acted quickly this time and hit the accelerator hard. Meanwhile, Yossi had come out of the house, and I could now see him lifting his gun and firing a shot.

"No, you don't!" I screamed inside my car as I rushed toward the low picket fence in front of me. I raced the car straight through it, pieces of white fence flying in the air around me, then drove onto the grass field, bumping toward Tristan and Kimmie, who were running for their lives, ducking as the shots were fired behind them. They heard my car as I smashed through the fence, then stopped and stared as I raced up on their side and waved like a crazy woman while rolling down the window and unlocking the doors, signaling for them to get in. Kimmie didn't think twice. She grabbed the handle in the back and pulled the door open, then pushed her son inside. Tristan tumbled into the back seat, and I told him to keep his head down.

"Hurry! Get in!" I yelled at Kimmie as I spotted Yossi coming up behind them, running across the grass. I could see the coldness in his eyes as he lifted the gun again, aimed at Kimmie's back while she struggled to get in.

A shot was fired, and Kimmie screamed. She fell flat onto the backseat.

I looked at Yossi as he stood still for a few seconds, then grabbed for his chest, where blood was gushing out. Then I looked down at my own hand and the gun I had instinctively pulled from my purse, then fired.

Tristan reached over and pulled the door closed while I stepped on it once again, and the car bumped back onto the road, leaving no trace of us behind except for the dust lingering in the air.

Part IV

THREE DAYS LATER

Chapter 49

"You have to call the school. They're calling every day."

My mom was annoyed on the other end. I could tell by the way she breathed heavily between words.

"You missed the meeting with the principal," she continued, and I could hear in her tone that she wanted to add, *who does that? What kind of a mother doesn't come when the principal wants to talk to you about your child?*

I knew how my mother felt, and I understood why she felt that way because I hadn't told her what I was doing or why I hadn't returned. How could I? I'd only endanger her as well as my children. It was better that she didn't know anything at all.

We had been hiding for three days and not told a soul what was happening. I hadn't even called Isabella to let her know that I was with Kimmie and her son. I couldn't get the thought out of my mind that somehow they had a leak in the FBI. How else did Yossi keep showing up? How did he know where to find Kimmie? How did he even know she was alive? I wasn't taking any chances.

I had gotten rid of my cell phone and thrown it in the trash close to the farmhouse in case they tried to track us down that way—if they were tapping my home phone. I had planned ahead and brought a big pile of cash just in case. I had bought a bunch of burner phones that I used to call home twice a day, checking on the kids. I used a new one every time just to be safe, and I drove away from the motel where we were staying, so they wouldn't be able to find us by the cell tower the call went through.

As I said, I wasn't taking any chances.

"It's gonna be okay, Mom. Just tell them I'm out of town, and I will hopefully be back soon. I'll meet with him once I get back."

My mom snorted. "I've already arranged a meeting with the principal tomorrow. I'll go and talk to him and try to sort things out, now that you refuse to be an adult and take care of your son's school."

I went quiet. I was kind of relieved since the last thing I could think about right now was what kind of trouble my son had gotten himself into, but at the same time, I felt so guilty it almost ate me up.

"When will you be home?" my mom asked.

"I can't say yet," I said. "It might be a few more days. At least."

"A few more days?" my mom said. "You can't be serious, Eva Rae. I have a life too, you know. You can't just expect me to throw out everything I have planned every time you need to go away..."

"Mom, I wouldn't ask this of you if it weren't important. You know this."

She went quiet, then grumbled. "Okay, then. I'll stay for a couple more days if it's really that important."

"It is," I said with a relieved sigh. "Thanks, Mom. Kiss the kids for me. I'll call again later and say goodnight."

I hung up, then stared at the burner phone before taking out the battery and throwing it in the trash bin next to me. Then I got back inside the car and took off. I drove for a few minutes down the street before I spotted the sign of the small motel where we were staying for the night. Kimmie and Tristan were waiting inside the room. Tomorrow, we'd be in a new motel in a new town. That had been our lives for the past few days.

As I said, I wasn't taking any chances.

Chapter 50

THEN:

"THAT'S AN EXCELLENT STORY, SAM."

Jacob, who was the editor of the day, looked at her from above his glasses. Everyone in the conference room nodded in agreement, even the older journalists, who usually didn't give Samantha the time of day since she was, after all, nothing but an intern.

She had just presented her story, the one she had been working on for two weeks, putting in more hours than what seemed humanly possible. It was the story of the mayor of Washington, Peter Bounik, and how he had raked in half a million dollars from consultants who he then helped attain lucrative contracts with the city.

"I say it's so good we run it as today's top," Jacob added. "And Samantha will finish it and see her own byline in the news tonight."

Samantha couldn't breathe. She stared at him, barely able to swallow. The top story? Tonight's top story?

Had she heard him right?

If so, then that had never happened to an intern before. She felt like she could explode with excitement. It was way more than what Sam had dared to hope for. All she had the nerve to dream of was researching it, and then maybe one of the older journalists would take over and make sure it was aired. She would know it was her story while he'd get the credit, but that was usually how these things went —especially with a story as big as this.

"Are you sure about this?" Mitt Paige, the anchor, said, leaning forward. "I mean, no offense to Sam, who is and will be a great journalist, but to take a chance on an intern? For tonight's top story?"

Jacob sent him a smile, then folded his hands on top of his papers. "I know what I'm doing, Mitt. Sam here will prove to us what she's made of."

Sam felt how she almost grew ten inches taller as all eyes were on her. She most certainly would prove to Jacob that she was worth him taking a chance on her. He was not going to regret it.

Just as Sam thought this to herself, the door to the conference room opened, and someone walked inside. As he did, the room fell silent. Sam lifted her gaze and felt her heart drop. Julianna, another intern sitting next to her, leaned over and whispered:

"What's Wanton doing here?"

Sam stared at him, feeling her face flush as their eyes met, and she saw nothing but coldness in his.

"Carry on," he said, addressed to Jacob. He closed the door behind him, then leaned against the wall while observing them. Sam didn't dare to look up and see if he was looking at her or not. It felt like he was.

"O-okay," Jacob said. "We were just talking about today's top story, researched by our very bright intern, Samantha over here," Jacob said and smiled at her, looking almost like a proud dad. "And how we have decided to let her finish the story and get her name on the screen tonight. We were also talking about letting her do a live following her report. She has such a pretty face that deserves to be on television."

Samantha lowered her eyes as Wanton turned to look at her while Jacob told him the story's details. She felt his eyes scrutinizing her and felt sick to her stomach. A long silence followed—one that made her want to scream.

"I don't think that's such a good idea," Wanton then said.

"Excuse me?" Jacob said.

Wanton shook his head. "I'm sure Samantha here is an excellent journalist, but she isn't ready for a story like that. It's too big for her. I say Irene finishes it. She'll do it the justice it deserves."

"But...I..." Sam burst out, but then stopped herself.

Wanton's eyes felt like knives of ice on her body.

"Yes?"

"It's just that...I worked hard on it, sir, and I know I can finish it."

Their eyes locked, and she felt like she had to throw up. His were harsh and angry, and like he couldn't hate her more. It made her feel so small.

He shook his head with a tsk. "Yeah, I don't think so. You're only an intern. Learn to know your place."

With that, he turned around and left. Sam sat there, feeling herself blush with anger and humiliation.

"Sorry, Sam," Jacob said on their way out after the meeting had ended. "I know you could do it, but Wanton is my boss. There really isn't anything else I can do."

She left the conference room and walked to her computer to get all her research ready to hand over to Irene, who would get the entire credit for this story of a lifetime. She sat down with a deep sigh, pressing back tears when a private message appeared on her screen.

It was from Wanton.

YOU NEED TO BE CAREFUL.

She stared at it, her heart hammering in her chest. What was this? What was he trying to tell her?

She wrote back:

WHY?

A pause followed before the answer came:

YOU WOULDN'T WANT ANYONE TO KNOW WHAT YOU'VE BEEN UP TO.

Sam stared at the words, unable to focus properly. She didn't like the sound of what he was saying. What she had been up to? Did he mean with him? That they had been together? Was that what he was saying she had to be careful of? That no one found out? Or what was he talking about?

WHAT DO YOU MEAN?

Another message appeared right away:

WE NEED TO MAKE SURE THERE'S A JOB FOR YOU HERE WHEN YOU'RE DONE, RIGHT?

Sam could barely breathe as she looked at the screen. What on earth was all this? Was he threatening her to keep silent? Was he saying that if anyone found out she had been with him, then she wouldn't be able to get a job?

She sank back in her chair, feeling suddenly scared. Had she ruined her own chances by sleeping with the boss? Was this going to cling to her for the rest of her career? Had she ruined everything for herself before it had even begun?

Chapter 51

"How long are we going to live like this?"

Kimmie glared at me across the car. We had left the rental car on the side of the road back in Sykesville and then hitchhiked to the nearest town, where I had found a car dealer that sold me an old beat-up Dodge Caravan for six hundred dollars cash. It didn't run well and wasn't going to last us more than a couple of weeks, but it was cheap and untraceable, so it was the way to go. Now, we were scrambling along the road, old fast-food bags on the floors, half-drunken sodas in the cup holders. The seats were greasy and sticky, and it was freezing inside the van since the heat didn't work.

I looked at Kimmie. We had been on the run for four days now and living in tight spaces, constantly looking over each other's shoulders. It was driving us all nuts.

"I mean, what's your plan, Eva Rae?" she continued with a deep groan. "You must have a plan of some sort, right?"

I didn't. But I couldn't really admit to that. For now, the plan was to keep them both safe. The trial was three days away, and Wanton had to be desperate to get rid of Kimmie by now. If I could keep her alive until the trial started, then maybe we had a chance. But no, I didn't have a plan, not a detailed one at least.

"We are going to spend the night at a Motel 6 tonight," I said and took a right turn. "That's the plan."

"You don't have any plan, do you?" Kimmie said and looked out the window. "I can't stand living like this."

"At least you get to sleep in a bed at night," I said. "You're lucky I always bring a stash of cash for emergencies like these. Otherwise, they would be breathing down your neck by now."

"I hate those lousy motels," she said. "I hate them. They're so dirty and filled with bugs, and ugh. I can't stand the noisy AC that keeps turning off and on all night. It wakes me up constantly. I need a good night's sleep!"

I exhaled, then stopped at a red light. A police car drove past us on the other side, then turned down a smaller road. My heart skipped a beat as it did every time I saw one. We couldn't trust anyone at this point if someone from inside the FBI was involved.

"Listen, Kimmie. This isn't exactly my ideal situation either. Up until a few weeks ago, I dreamed of seeing you dead. Every waking hour of the day, I wanted to kill you myself for what you did to me. And now, I'm trying to save your sorry butt while my family is missing me at home. Do you think I want to be here?"

She turned to face me, then looked down at her fingers. "No. Of course not. I...I just get so frustrated because I feel like...well, I keep thinking I should just have kept my mouth shut. I should never have told you the truth about what happened in that apartment. If I hadn't, then I wouldn't be in this screwed-up situation right now. I would be at home with my son, living our normal lives. I keep asking myself, why did I have to do it? Why couldn't I just have lied?"

The light turned green, but I didn't go. I stared at her, mouth open.

"Because you have an obligation," I said. "A responsibility to Samantha and so many other women. If you didn't speak up, no one would be able to stop Wanton. He'd just continue on and on screwing with people's lives. He's a bastard, and we both know it. You think he only did what he did to you? That he only treated you that way? Asking you to sleep with him in exchange for a job? Then, you are very naïve. He's most likely done the same to many others who didn't dare to speak up. And he will continue if no one dares to take a risk as you have. You have a responsibility to speak up for the coming generation's sake. So these things won't happen again. That's why you did it. And that's why I'm keeping you alive, so you can do it again once the trial starts. I'm not concerned about your life, but for my daughters' sake. I want them to grow up in a better world than we did. Will it be easy? No. No one said it would be. It doesn't mean you shouldn't have done it."

Kimmie stared at me, eyes wide, tears welling up.

"Now, I won't hear you complain one more time, or I will leave you to guys like Yossi; do you hear me?"

Kimmie never answered. She turned her head away and became quiet the rest of the way to the motel.

Chapter 52

He walked in on her, sitting at his laptop in his office. John saw the empty bottle of white wine on the desk in front of her and the glass in her hand and knew she was in a bad state. Carol looked up at him, her eyes unfocused.

He slammed the door shut behind him.

Carol jumped, startled.

"What do you think you're doing?"

She shook her head, then finished her glass of wine.

"You bastard."

John rubbed his forehead intensely, preparing himself for this, trying to remain calm. His anger had been one of the issues he had to work on when trying to save his marriage, but it was easier said than done. He stepped forward.

"Carol, you're not feeling well. Let me get you to bed. Come."

He reached out for her hand, but she pulled it away with an angry snort. "You can't keep doing this to me. Do you hear me?"

"Please, Carol. You've been drinking. Let's talk in the morning. I have a ton of work I need to get done before bedtime."

That made Carol laugh. It was a mocking laugh that soon turned into sad sobbing. "You have work to do, huh? Let me guess. For Wanton, huh? Do you have to do work for your little boyfriend, huh?"

"Let me get you to bed, Carol, before you say something you'll regret tomorrow. We talked about this. We shouldn't have these conversations when you've been drinking. We can talk about it in the..."

He reached for her arm again and grabbed it, but she pulled away. "Don't touch me, you bastard. You don't think I know what you and Wanton have been up to, huh? You don't think I know what's going on?"

John clenched his fist in anger. He spoke through gritted teeth. "Carol. I told you. What happened was once. It stopped. You have to trust me. We can't keep doing this to one another. You have to start trusting me."

"Trust you? Ha! That's a good one. How can I trust you when you keep lying to me, huh?"

As she said the words, she turned the laptop so John could look at the screen. He stared at the picture of Samantha Durkin, first overwhelmed by deep sadness, then anger filling his body.

"You told me you barely knew her. What's her picture doing on your laptop, then? In your private photos?"

John clenched his jaws, unable to contain his anger. This time, she had gone too far. He reached over and closed the lid of the laptop.

"Answer me, John," Carol said, getting up on her feet but staggering as she tried to stand still and look into his eyes. Hers were wet and glossy, and he could tell she had been crying.

John stared at her, nostrils flaring. Carol slammed her hand onto the desk, making the small statue his daughter had made of clay for Christmas clatter.

"Talk to me, darn it, John. Why do you have a picture on your computer of the girl that Wanton killed?"

He stared at her, unable to speak, anger boiling inside him.

"Answer me, John! Or I swear I'll...I'll leave you now. I'll go to our room, pack my suitcase, and leave. Right now."

He shrugged with a snort. He didn't have the strength to have this fight again. "Then go, Carol. No one is forcing you to stay."

Her eyes met his. Hers wore a surprise to them.

"So...that's it? You're not even going to fight anymore? You're not even going to try and defend yourself?"

"I have been fighting, Carol. I have been fighting for so long I can barely remember a time when we didn't. But I can't do it anymore. Now, will you please leave? I have work to do."

She gave him a look of disgust, then snorted as she walked past him:

"I'll leave you to do your...work. I'll leave you with your girlfriend, Wanton. Maybe you should have married him instead of me, huh? It seems like you're willing to do anything to keep him happy, even if it means making your own wife miserable."

Without thinking, John took a step forward, lifted his hand in the air, then stopped himself, hand stuck in mid-air.

Carol stared at him, eyes wide, fear struck on her face. As she saw the hand stop, she composed herself.

"Go ahead," she said with sudden defiance. "Hit me, John. I will go to the police and tell them what you did. That will only make the divorce easier on my part once I get ahold of my lawyer. Maybe I'll tell them to take a look at your computer as well, huh? I have a feeling the police will be interested to know you have the picture of the dead girl on your computer. Don't you? For all they know, you could have murdered her. I lied for you about your whereabouts that night. I told them we were together, but we both know that isn't the truth, right? I haven't asked questions because I promised you that I'd trust you from now on, but now I'm asking. Where were you the night that girl fell from Wanton's penthouse? Did you kill her?"

John lowered his hand, realizing he was letting his anger run away with him. He needed to compose himself.

"You will not talk to the police," he simply said, running the hand through his hair. "Because if you do, I will make sure you never see the children again."

"Oh, yeah? And just who do you think the court will give them to, huh? Me or a murderer?"

"Get out," he said and pointed at the door. He then grabbed his laptop and threw it at the wall behind her while screaming at the top of his lungs:

"GET OUT!"

Chapter 53

I popped open a bottle of Merlot I had bought in a little market that we stopped by on our way. I found two plastic cups in the bathroom, wrapped in plastic, and poured myself a glass. I looked at Kimmie, sitting on the bed next to me. Tristan was watching TV from the other bed. Kimmie hadn't said a word to me since I told her off in the car.

"Do you want a glass?" I asked.

She didn't look up at me, just kept staring at her fingers.

"Kimmie?"

I stared at her, then sighed. I sat at the foot of her bed.

"Kimmie? Do you want a glass of wine?"

She lifted her gaze and met mine, then nodded. I poured her one into the other plastic cup, then handed it to her. Her eyes avoided mine as she took it. I drank from mine while observing her.

"Listen, I'm sorry if I was too harsh on you back there. I got carried away."

She didn't look at me, so I continued.

"It's just...well, to be honest, I really admire what you did. You standing up for yourself and telling me your story required a lot of courage. I know who it is you're up against, and doing what you did was extremely brave of you. I think that's why I want you to be proud of yourself and not feel guilty for it or regret it."

That made Kimmie lift her gaze and look into my eyes.

"I think you're ashamed of yourself," I continued. "Of what you have done because you were in the apartment in the first place to get a job, and you're beating yourself up over it. You feel bad for having told me what happened because of the consequences it has come with. But I need you to drop that. It'll get you nowhere. The guy killed a young woman; he hurt you and tried to have you killed. He deserves to go to jail, or he will just do it again. And others will see him get away with it and think they can do stuff like that too. You're doing something very important here, Kimmie. It's one thing to speak up against a powerful man, but to speak up against someone who is also a public person, that's an entirely different kind of beast. I need you to be proud of yourself for it."

Kimmie's eyes stared into mine, and I smiled. I lifted my glass and tapped it against hers.

"I want you to own it. You're badass, Kimmie, and I want you to tell yourself that. Or I'll have to rename you from now on. Kick-ass Kimmie will be your name."

That made her chuckle.

"I guess I can drink to that," she said. "Kick-ass Kimmie."

We both sipped our wine. It didn't taste very good, but it wasn't too bad given the circumstances—it kind of fit somehow.

A silence grew between us. Kimmie fiddled with the plastic cup between her fingers while I took a couple of sips more from mine. Tristan was watching a very loud game show on TV.

"But you're right," Kimmie finally said. "Telling you what happened was the hardest thing I ever had to do. I hate myself for going with him up to that apartment, and I keep thinking that if only I hadn't...then, well, maybe that girl would be alive, and maybe my life wouldn't be like this. I can't believe I fell for it and went with him."

"It wasn't the first time, was it?" I asked.

She looked down and shook her head. "We had an ongoing thing back in the day—when I was a reporter, and he was a news director."

"An affair?"

She scoffed. "I wouldn't even call it that. It wasn't like he took me out to dinner or even asked me where I was from."

"So, just sex."

She shrugged. "Times were different back then. It was just the way it was. No one questioned it. Today, the young generation does. They know how to speak up for themselves better. I guess a lot of people just had enough, you know? It's been going on for way too long. It was time for someone to stand up, you know?"

"I have deep respect for the fact that you did," I said.

Kimmie nodded and sipped her wine. "I just wish it didn't have such big consequences for all three of us."

I wrinkled my forehead. "What do you mean...all three?"

Kimmie's eyes became wide. "You know, Samantha and me and...Tristan."

Chapter 54

Rachel's hands were shaking as she sat down in the restaurant. She was the first one there and ordered a glass of wine right away. She had taken a double dose of Prozac this morning, upping her dose to the maximum in order to get through the day. Now, as the waiter brought her the wine, she gulped it down so fast it almost hurt her throat, then asked for another one. She fiddled nervously with the glass, tapping her fingers on it while waiting for the others to arrive.

She almost hadn't come. When she woke up this morning, she had felt such deep anxiety that she had felt sure she would die. Her heart had beaten so fast, it had hurt her chest, and she had to sit down because she was so dizzy. Now, she felt like it was happening again. Her fingers were buzzing, the room spinning, and she felt her breaths getting shorter.

Easy, now. You can do it. Just breathe, Rachel. Deep long breaths. The wine and medicine will kick in soon and make you relax.

Rachel closed her eyes and tried to calm herself. She kept telling herself she was doing something good—for future generations. She was not doing this for herself, but because it mattered—because it was important.

So it wouldn't happen to someone else.

"Rachel!"

She opened her eyes and looked at Crystal. She was flanked by two other women, looking every bit as anxious and scared as Rachel felt. Rachel wanted to run away, just pick up her purse and walk out of there.

"Okay, girls, go ahead and sit down. Rachel, this is Olivia, and this is Winnie."

Rachel forced a smile and nodded at them. They shared a gaze for a few seconds before they sat down. She could see the anxiety in both of them and knew exactly how they felt.

"I see you've already gotten some wine," Crystal said with a soft smile. "I'll order some more. Let's have a couple of bottles. We girls need it, huh?"

Rachel nodded nervously, then emptied the second glass. The wine was beginning to do its magic in her along with the medicine, and soon she felt calmer. She had been so worried about this meeting, but these girls seemed to be just as scared as her, and they didn't seem to judge her in any way.

"Winnie, how about you begin? You tell the other girls your story," Crystal said as the wine had arrived and they had ordered entrees.

Winnie looked flustered into her wine. She gave Crystal a nervous smile, then started.

"I had been at WBC News for about a week when Richard Wanton stuck his head inside my editing suite. He was the news director back then; it was like seventeen years ago. When he came in, he said he wanted to welcome me and told me that I needed to meet with my new colleagues and that they were a group of people meeting up at a bar not far from the station after work. I could just stop by once I was done for the day and say hi. Get to know everyone. I was, of course, very flattered—Richard Wanton, the former anchor and now news director, asking me to come out and meet up with other journalists. I was young and new, and it was a dream for me. Of course, I'd come."

Winnie paused and drank from her wine.

"But what happened when you got there?" Crystal asked. "You can tell them. We've all been there."

Winnie nodded, then swallowed. "When I got there, it was just Wanton and his close friend John Savage, who later became the news director of the network when Wanton became the CEO of the news department of the entire network. Those two have looked after one another always and covered for one another. Anyway, he was there too, and I thought it was very strange that there was no one else. They told me no one else could make it, and I believed them and sat down. We got a couple of beers, and along the way, I soon realized that they had ordered a hotel room for the three of us and that it was expected that I go with them there."

Rachel almost choked on her wine when hearing this.

"I got up and hurried away," Winnie said. "I didn't want any of that because I was married and just had my first child. But this meant my career was pretty much tanked after that. I never got the good stories again and never was promoted. When I wanted to become a live reporter, I went to Wanton's office, and he told me that I would have the job in a month. And within that same month, we'd have slept together."

Rachel stared at her, barely breathing as tears piled up in Winnie's eyes. "I didn't know what to do."

Winnie paused again and used a napkin to wipe her eyes. "So...I did it. And I have hated myself for it ever since. A few months later, I had to quit because I couldn't stand it anymore. I told my husband, and we decided we had to move far away. I stopped working as a reporter and found another job. I could no longer work in this business. It had been ruined for me."

"It's okay," Crystal said and placed a hand on top of Winnie's. She smiled gently at her and looked into her eyes. "We've all been there. All of us around this table have tried this on our own bodies.

But we're done keeping quiet about it, right? Telling each other our stories serves to help us tell our own, and only that way can we get the courage to speak up and hopefully stop this from happening again. It's unpleasant to do, but someone has to be the first, right?"

Rachel nodded, finally breathing again, feeling how the tension in her body eased up, how her shoulders came down, and her pounding heart was calmed down for the first time in a very long time. Hearing Winnie's story made it easier for her to tell her story again, and she soon did, feeling great relief not to be alone, almost uplifted even. Like telling it made her free of the burden it had become inside of her. They were now a small flock of women doing this together. She wasn't alone anymore. And for the first time, she actually believed they could make a difference.

They ended the dinner by encouraging each other and a big group hug. Then, Crystal pulled out a phone and took a picture of all of them sitting together at the table. One she said that would remind them of how it all began.

"Once this really goes down, and we go public with it, you'll look back at this moment and remember how scared you felt, then be proud of yourself for not backing down even when faced with that fear. That, my girls, is real courage."

Chapter 55

Kimmie's eyes were avoiding mine. It was obvious she was hiding something. I stared at her, scrutinizing her every move. She grabbed the wine bottle and poured herself some more, then gulped down a big portion. She lifted the plastic cup to drink more when I placed my hand on her arm.

She lifted her glare to look at me.

"There was someone else there," I said.

Kimmie lowered her eyes to her plastic cup, then drank from it again—big sips that she swallowed fast.

"In the apartment," I continued.

She didn't look at me but emptied her cup and filled it up again. The bottle was shaking in her hand as she poured from it.

"Kimmie," I said. "Who else was there?"

She shook her head. "No one."

"You talked about three people, and I don't think you meant Tristan. You were talking about someone else. Who?"

"I don't know what you're talking about," Kimmie said and drank again. Her words were getting slurred; she was tipsy now.

"Yes, you do. Of course, you do. You need to tell me this now, Kimmie."

"Why? It doesn't change anything."

"Yes, it does. It changes everything. Are you kidding me? We need to tell the FBI about this person. We're talking about a possible witness to murder here, don't you see? We're about to go to trial. I don't understand why you'd not tell us about this?"

I paused and sipped my cup.

"Unless this person won't support your story, of course," I added. "Is that why you haven't told us?"

Kimmie shook her head. She was getting desperate now; I could tell by her fingers fiddling with the cup.

"But I don't think that is why, Kimmie. I think you're covering for this person for another reason, am I right?"

Kimmie bit the side of her cheek, then nodded.

I threw out my hands. "So, you've been lying about this. How am I going to protect you if you're lying to me? I thought you told me everything that happened in that apartment. What else did you hide from me?"

Kimmie drank, emptied her cup, then poured the rest of the bottle into it. She emptied it, then tried to stand up, but almost fell as she did and had to lean on the nightstand.

"Kimmie, where are you going?"

"To get more wine," she said and lifted the empty bottle, almost tipping it over. "We're out."

"No, you're not running out on me now," I said. "We need to talk about this. I need to know who this person was. Could it be a possible witness?"

Kimmie paused and looked down at me. Her eyes were glossy.

"I...I..."

"Kimmie, come on. Just tell me who it is."

She shook her head. "I...I gotta go get this..."

Then, she hurried toward the door.

"Kimmie, stop!"

She paused by the door, hand on the handle.

"Kimmie, you can't go anywhere. You might be seen."

She scoffed, turned the handle, and opened the door, then stormed outside.

Chapter 56

THEN:

He was ignoring her. For weeks, he had avoided her looks and not even smiled at her when accidentally meeting her in the hallways at the TV station. He had written no messages to her and didn't call anymore. Sam had thought it would feel like a relief, that this was what she wanted, but somehow, it filled her with this strange anxiousness. Especially every time she saw him. Wanton's coldness and silence toward her made her feel like she had done something wrong —like she had messed up. She had come to like his messages that always opened with "hi, gorgeous." And career-wise, things were going downhill. She was no longer getting any stories, and the ones she tried to push through with were shot down just as fast as she was able to present them. She never got any credit for the mayor story, even though it became a big deal, one that people still talked about. No one knew it had been hers, and they never would. Samantha was beginning to fear that she had ruined her own career.

One night, she was at a party with some of Nat's friends, and she was sitting on the couch while most others were dancing. She was staring at her phone while the music blasted loudly around her. She had been drinking a lot, maybe a little too much, and now, she felt sad. She wondered why it bothered her so much, why Wanton's silence made her feel this way.

Then she did something silly. She called him.

"Hello?"

His voice sounded cheerful.

"Hi. It's Samantha."

Deep silence. Samantha felt her heart drop.

The next thing he said came out almost screaming:

"No!"

Then he hung up.

Samantha stared at the display of the phone, her hand shaking heavily. What had she done? He had always told her she couldn't call him or even email him since his secretary read through those. She could only write to him in the messaging system where the messages disappeared as soon as you had read them. Everything else was too dangerous. As she sat there, she knew she had messed up. Big time. She felt sick to her stomach.

Without saying anything to Nat, she left the party and walked home. As she strolled through the streets in the pouring rain, her phone suddenly rang. She pulled it out and saw that it was him. She picked it up.

"H-hello!"

"Don't you ever do that again. I told you never to call me. My wife was right next to me. She could have heard it."

"I...I'm sorry...I was at a party and it...was an accident. Some people were playing around with my phone and accidentally called you. I'm so sorry."

He went quiet, then chuckled. "I don't buy that. It's okay. You got drunk. It happens. But don't lie to me. You're too good a girl to lie. Don't let it happen again. Ever. Okay?"

"O-okay."

They hung up. Samantha ran home in the rain, feeling the embarrassment eating her up from the inside. It was the worst feeling in the world. How could she have been so stupid? She had ruined everything. She was just a worthless creature who had made such a mess of her own life.

Chapter 57

I jumped down from the bed and ran after Kimmie. Tristan sat up and called for his mom to come back while I sprang for the door.

"Kimmie, come back here!"

As I stepped outside, I saw her running across the parking lot, swaying slightly. I took off after her. She wasn't running very fast, so I caught up to her quickly.

"Leave me alone," she hissed and tried to push me away.

I grabbed her shoulder and made her stop. "Come on, Kimmie. Come back, and we can talk."

"I don't want to talk to you anymore."

"Okay, then don't talk. Just come back to the room."

Kimmie sighed. Tears were welling up in her eyes again. She grabbed a lock of my hair and put it behind my ear. "I can't tell you who it is. I just can't, okay?"

"Can you tell me why you're covering for this person?"

She shook her head, then looked down. "I have my reasons."

"It's not because he's threatening you? Because he could be an accomplice to murder, you do realize that, right?"

That made her look up at me, her eyes terrified. "Oh, no, it's not that. This person would never...I mean, of course, I can understand what you mean, but...it's John..."

Kimmie paused. I stared at her, secretly noting that she had just given me the first name. I turned my head to see what had caught her eye. A black car was driving by on the street, going very slow. As it came closer, someone rolled down the windows.

I reacted fast. I threw myself on top of Kimmie as the shots fell.

Pop-pop-pop!

We landed on the asphalt, me on top of her. Kimmie screamed in my ear as the car continued past us. I lifted my eyes to look at the license plate but couldn't see much except for the letters ED. Then I jumped up, grabbed Kimmie, and pulled her to her feet.

"We need to get out of here, fast."

"Who...what was that?" Kimmie yelled at me with fear stuck in her throat. "How...how did they find us?"

"I have to figure that out, but first, we need to get out of here."

We rushed inside the motel and grabbed the little stuff we had, like my weekend bag, computer, and purse, and a couple of bags with snacks. Tristan was sitting on the bed, shaking, as we told him we had to leave. We walked cautiously into the parking lot, where I saw the black car come back toward us.

"Quick, we need to go out in the back."

We hurried around the corner and ran around the building.

"But what about the car?" Kimmie said, panting. "It's parked that way."

"We have to leave it," I said. "Continue on foot."

The black car leaped into the parking lot and approached us, its headlights hitting our car.

"But...?"

"Now, Kimmie. GO!"

Chapter 58

"Things are starting to shape up."

Rachel stared at her husband and daughter, sitting at the table eating the breakfast she had prepared for them. She had just grabbed a cup of coffee for herself when Crystal called. Rachel walked away from them, so they wouldn't listen in. She still hadn't told Joe about what she had been up to. She kept postponing it. She had almost told him a few times, but every time she started to, something always came up, a phone call, or she chickened out.

"Really? What does that mean?" she asked Crystal while she walked into the guest bedroom and closed the door.

"We have a meeting set up. With John Savage."

Rachel wrinkled her forehead. "John Savage? The news director?"

"Yes. I just spoke with him today."

"Really?"

"Yes, the plan is we will meet with him and tell him our stories. He wants to hear them."

"I... I don't understand. Isn't he like Wanton's right hand and best friend?"

"Yes. But he has agreed to meet with us and hear the stories."

"But...why?"

"He's on our side," Crystal said. "He wants to help."

Rachel sat down on the bed, feeling confused, anxiety starting to rise in the pit of her stomach.

"I...I don't know what to say."

"Just say you'll be there. With a man like John Savage on our side, we have a much better chance at getting somewhere."

"But...shouldn't we be getting lawyers? If we're starting a case?"

Crystal laughed. "Of course. We're working on that part too. All in due time. But for now, it's all about gathering as many on our side as possible, right?"

"I...don't know," Rachel said. "You tell me. It's not like I've done this type of thing before."

"Neither have I. But just promise me you'll be there, please?"

Rachel cleared her throat. "Of course. If it can help in any way."

"Great! I'll text you the details, address and time to be there and so on. See you soon then."

"Wait."

"Yes?"

"What's in it for John Savage? Why is he doing this?"

Crystal went quiet for a few seconds. "My guess is that he wants Wanton's job. He's been right underneath him for many years, and now he wants his place in the sun. That would be my best guess."

Rachel nodded. It sounded plausible. "Okay, then. Thank you."

"See you soon."

Rachel hung up and stared at the display of her phone. Her hands were shaking slightly still. It was the name from her past that had her feeling anxious again. John Savage had been her closest boss back when Wanton raped her. She hadn't told him what happened because she simply didn't think he would do anything. It was commonly known that those two were best friends and had known each other since college. She had never thought he would ever betray the man who made him who he was.

But that just showed you that you never really knew someone until they had the chance to stab you in the back.

Rachel walked out as her husband and daughter were about to leave for work and school. She kissed them both, handed Marissa her lunch, then waved at them, feeling uplifted and excited. Things really were shaping up for them now. A man like Savage was a powerful man. With him on their side, there was no stopping them.

They were about to make history.

Chapter 59

We continued on foot, walking for most of the night. I kept watching for the black car, worried that these people would catch up to us. Around three o'clock, Kimmie sat down on the asphalt and started to cry.

"I can't keep going anymore. I just can't."

I wanted to tell her to pull herself back up, to get it together, but I was too tired for that. Instead, I sank down next to her with a deep sigh. Tristan laid in the grass next to us, groaning loudly.

"How do they keep finding us?" Kimmie said after catching her breath. "How do they know where I am?"

"These are highly-trained killers," I said. "At least the guy I shot back in Sykesville was. He was a former Mossad agent. You can hire people like him if you have enough money. And if there is anything Wanton has, it's that. Connections and money."

Kimmie moaned, annoyed. "I am sick of this. There are still two days until the trial starts. Will we have to keep running until then? And will we ever make it back?"

"We will. But you're right about one thing," I said. "Even the most highly trained soldiers need a way to track someone. There must be some way they're finding you. And it can't be facial recognition because we've stayed clear of any surveillance cameras. I made sure of that."

"But then, how?"

I turned my head and looked at Tristan, who was half asleep in the grass next to us while the cars rushed by on the highway.

"Give me your boots," I said.

Tristan sat up. "Excuse me?"

"I need your boots," I said and approached his feet. I grabbed the right one and pulled it off, then grabbed my flashlight from my weekend bag and turned it on. I examined the boot closely, then looked at him, lighting up his face. He lifted his hands and covered himself from the bright light.

"The other one, please."

"Okay, okay."

He pulled it off and handed it to me. "Here you go."

I shone the light on it, examining the sole, then looked inside it, putting a finger under the inside sole, pulling it up the sides, but found nothing.

"Huh. I was so certain."

I gave Tristan the shoes back, then looked at his arms as he tied his shoes. Then, I turned to look at Kimmie.

"Are you wearing a fitness tracker?"

She nodded and showed me her wrist. "A Fitbit. I use it to track how many steps I walk every day. You know—to make sure I get my ten thousand in."

"Is the Bluetooth turned on?" I asked.

"I think so. I haven't really thought about it."

I grabbed her wrist, then took the band off. "Then, that's how they're tracking us. It's the easiest thing in the world. All you need is an app. Anyone can do it."

"Wow," Kimmie said. "I didn't know that. I haven't charged it since we were at the house back in Sykesville, but it lasts up to five days without a charge."

I felt the band in my hand, then threw it into the bushes.

"Well, now it'll die out here."

I grabbed my bag, then swung it over my shoulder. "But it won't be long before they track us to this place, so we should keep moving."

Chapter 60

We walked most of the night, then found a rest area where we used the restrooms, making sure to pull up our hoodies and jackets to cover our faces from the surveillance cameras. I then pulled out a burner phone and called my dad.

"I need your help with something."

"You in trouble, kid?" he asked, trying to sound fatherly. It always took me by surprise since I hadn't known him most of my life while growing up. We had reconnected late in life after I forgave him for kidnapping my sister and taking her away from me for my entire childhood. It wasn't something I had done easily, and I was still working on accepting him acting like a father. He was a very skilled hacker who worked for big cybersecurity companies, at least that's what he told me. I had a feeling I didn't really want to know what he did for a living, but I would come to him from time to time for help, and I sensed he enjoyed that.

"You can say that again. I can't tell you any details, but I need you to find out everything you can about a man named John Savage. Right now, he's the News Director of WBC News and Richard Wanton's right hand."

I figured it had to be him when Kimmie mentioned the name John. I knew him by reputation only, but he was a pretty big name in the media industry.

"John Savage, okay. And what do you want to know?"

I exhaled. "Just anything you can find. I suspect he played a role in killing the young girl who fell from the rooftop deck of Wanton's apartment a few weeks ago. Can you find his alibi for that night? Was he questioned during the investigation?"

"Okay, but why don't you ask Isabella Horne these questions? Weren't you working with her on this case?"

"It's a long story. I'm not sure I trust her or anyone inside the FBI right now. I'm not taking any chances that they find us again."

"Again? That doesn't sound good, Eva Rae. Are you sure you're safe?"

I looked around me as a white van drove up and parked not far from where I was standing. My heart started to pound in my chest. Was that them? Had they found us? Or maybe someone was watching me from the blue car parked in the corner?

A young couple jumped out and walked right past me. A black car drove up behind it and got my attention.

You're being paranoid, Eva Rae. Focus.

"What are you up to, Eva Rae?" My dad asked. "Are you okay?"

I exhaled. "I have to go. I'll call you another time, Dad. Just find me everything you can about the guy, okay?"

I hung up, thinking this was a mistake. There probably wasn't anything my dad could find that would help me find out if he was actually in the apartment or not. I needed to know his role in it and whether he was a witness or an accomplice. Somehow, I felt like he held the key I needed to find. But Kimmie wasn't talking anymore to me about it, and what I really needed to find out was why she was so keen on protecting him. Had he maybe threatened her? Did he have something on her to make her keep quiet about him being there?

Or was it something else entirely?

Kimmie and Tristan sat on a bench, and I threw out the burner phone in the trash bin, then walked toward them, wondering how I would solve this puzzle and keep them both safe at the same time.

How on earth will this ever end well?

I approached them as another car came toward us, and I felt my pulse quicken once again. Kimmie and Tristan had bought some snacks at a vending machine that they were eating, and I grabbed a Snickers bar, then chewed it fast while looking at them, then at the car that passed us at that instant.

"We should get moving," I said. "It's too dangerous to stay here."

"Where are we going?" Tristan asked as he got up. He was getting tired, and so was Kimmie. I had to find somewhere for us to stay soon. We all needed at least a couple of hours of sleep and a shower.

"I wish I knew," I said and grabbed my bag.

Chapter 61

THEN:

THEY WENT OUT AFTER WORK. It was just a small group of people, so Samantha thought it would be okay to say yes, even though she felt very insecure. For a few weeks, she had been focusing on her work, and only that, yet still felt like all eyes were on her. She believed she heard their whispering voices in the corners and by the coffee machine behind her back every day and was certain that everyone knew about her and Wanton.

Everyone knew, and everyone talked.

Wanton had started writing to her again. After she called him, he had begun writing sweet messages every day. He mostly commented on her outfit, telling her she looked cute or gorgeous, stuff like that. She had to admit, she enjoyed his attention, but she feared he wanted more than that. So, she stayed away from him as much as possible. It wasn't that hard since he wasn't often in the newsroom as he was mainly in the offices at the top of the building. But now and then, he peeked down to say hello, and then he'd smile and sometimes wink at her, making her blush.

The bar they usually went to after work was a small Irish pub around the corner from the building where they worked. They were just eight people going in, and she wasn't the only intern. Two others were with her, and she knew she could sit with them at the bar.

Samantha ordered a beer as she sat down with the other interns. That's when she spotted the News Director, John Savage, walk-in. He waved at some of the other journalists, then walked to sit with some of them. He smiled secretively at Samantha as he walked past the interns. It made her feel uncomfortable, and she lowered her eyes to avoid his.

"How's your story coming along?" One of the interns, Jacob, asked. "I heard you're working on something big? You're still a legend for that mayor story, at least among the interns, just so you know it."

That made Sam smile. She had received no recognition for that story, and even though that was the way it usually went for interns, it still bummed her out. Maybe because she was so close to actually getting to do it herself, getting her name on TV, and then it was taken away.

"Thanks," she said and sipped her beer, feeling uplifted. Maybe things weren't as bad as she made them out to be. Maybe people weren't only talking about her and Wanton; perhaps they actually saw what she was capable of? Maybe she had actually impressed them?

There's still hope. It's not all over yet.

"Hi there, Samantha, isn't it?"

Sam turned and saw John Savage. He had moved up and was now sitting next to her, smiling at her the same way he had when coming into the bar earlier. Sam swallowed hard. She tried to smile back. This guy would one day be the one to decide whether or not she'd be hired back after her internship. He was also Wanton's best friend since college.

"Yes, that's me."

"I know who you are. You've got quite the reputation around here."

"O-okay?"

"Oh, don't worry. I didn't mean that in a bad way at all. I know it was you who researched that story about Mayor Bounik. I know it was all your hard work."

That made Sam smile, relieved.

"Really?

John smiled back, then leaned over and whispered in her ear. "I know what happened with Wanton. Do you want to go somewhere private?"

Samantha stared at him, on the verge of breaking into tears. A deep furrow grew between John's eyes.

"What's wrong?"

He placed his hand on her shoulder, and the touch made her shiver. John leaned in. Samantha pulled away, grabbed her purse, and ran into the street, tears rolling down her cheeks.

Is that how they see me? Is that all I am to them?

Chapter 62

I had one more card to play. One I had been reluctant to pull out but would do if there was no other way. And we had reached that point now. There was no way back.

I had to call Miranda.

My ex-mother-in-law.

I used another burner phone, then told her where we were. We had stopped close to a BP gas station and a McDonald's on the other side. I didn't offer her any explanation; I just told her it was urgent, that I was in trouble. Miranda knew me well enough not to ask any more questions.

I had always liked Chad's mother and often thought about contacting her after the divorce. But somehow, I could never get myself to do it. It just felt odd somehow. Like I was no longer entitled to have her in my life.

She drove up twenty minutes later in her old purple 1987 Chevy Suburban pick-up truck and stopped. The sun had begun to rise behind the BP sign, and I felt exhausted.

"Eva Rae!"

She came out in her ripped jeans and a white T-shirt that read *Spiritual Gangster*. She grabbed me in a deep hug that almost lifted me off the ground, her silver mane flowing behind her back. Then she saw Kimmie, who was standing behind me. She dropped me, placed both hands on her hips, then said:

"What is *she* doing here?"

I exhaled. "She's the one I'm trying to protect."

"From what? Wrecking more homes? She's the one we need protection from if you ask me."

"She's a witness in the Wanton-trial in two days. They're trying to kill her."

Miranda gave me a puzzled look. "The what now?"

"You haven't heard about the Wanton trial?" I asked. "It's been all over the news the past several weeks."

"Honey, I don't follow the news as long as they don't follow me. I stopped watching that stuff many years ago and am only the happier for it. Can't trust anything that's being said anyway, am I right? It's all just fear-mongering. They want us afraid so that they can control us. That's just my two cents on that."

I nodded. I disagreed with her, but that didn't matter. The less she knew, the better anyway. She lived on a farm outside of a small town called Boonsboro, some sixty miles from D.C., and her place would be the perfect hideout for us until the trial. I just prayed I wasn't putting her in any danger by asking her for help.

"Someone is trying to kill her, you say?" Miranda asked and looked at Kimmie, who shifted on her feet nervously. Miranda laughed and faced me. "And it isn't you? Because no one would blame you for wanting to do that, hon. No one would even lift an eyebrow. The way she behaved, she's going to Hell on a full scholarship."

I looked at Kimmie, who seemed very uncomfortable. I couldn't blame her, yet I had to admit I enjoyed it just a little bit. That was okay, right?

"Come on," Miranda said. "Let's get you back to the farm and cleaned up. You look like you slept with the pigs and smell bad enough to gag a maggot. Now, get in. All of you."

Chapter 63

The upcoming trial was all over the news that very morning, again. Rachel stared at the TV in her kitchen while sipping her coffee, watching old footage of Richard Wanton walk out of the courtroom a free man some weeks ago when he was released on bail. The images of him glaring at the camera and smirking still aroused fear and anxiety in her, but this time, she felt stronger. She was terrified of what she was going to do, but at least she was no longer alone. She knew now that what had happened back then wasn't her fault, and it was time for them to stand up against the man.

The reporter stated that since the witness to the murder had been killed, it was a great likelihood that Wanton would be able to leave the courthouse in two days as a completely free man, cleared of all charges. The man who killed the witness was still on the loose but was believed to be a crazed fan of Wanton's, and during the investigation, the FBI had not found any connection to Wanton himself.

"With no witness and no hard evidence linking him to the murder of Samantha Durkin, it doesn't look like the FBI has much of a case left against Wanton," the reporter said, standing in front of the same courthouse in her gray suit jacket and skirt. Rachel remembered those days when she had been hopeful and aspiring like her, wanting to be a live reporter. Then she wondered how far this woman had to go to get to this position. How much had she had to bear to get to where she was today? How much weight, from sexual abuse or harassment, was she carrying around? What wasn't she telling her loved ones out of shame?

It was for women like her that Rachel was doing this. For her and the coming generations. Someone had to.

Rachel shook her head and turned off the TV. She finished her cup and grabbed her purse, then looked at her reflection in the mirror. She applied some lip gloss and corrected her eye makeup slightly. She looked good, better than she had in a long time, and she felt good about herself and what she was about to do.

She felt strong.

"You might get away with murder, but you won't escape us," she mumbled as she left the house and locked the front door. "The women you used, the ones you destroyed, we are still here, and there are many of us. And now, we're coming for you."

She got into her car, then drove across town until she reached an address in the expensive part of D.C. She drove through the gates as they opened after she had said her name into the intercom, then drove up the long driveway toward the mansion rising in front of her. She stopped the engine as she parked, then got out and walked up the stairs, where Crystal was waiting for her, holding her briefcase in her hand. She smiled when she saw her.

"Big day, huh? Are you ready? Winnie told her story yesterday, and it went really well."

Rachel nodded nervously, then looked up at the big glass front door that marked the entrance to the home of John Savage, News Director of WBC News.

"As ready as I will ever be, I guess."

"That's what I like to hear," Crystal said, then pressed the doorbell. It rang loud, and the sound cut into Rachel's bones, making her uneasy without understanding why.

Chapter 64

"Why did you call her? She hates me."

Kimmie stared at me as I came out of the bathroom. Kimmie and I were sharing a room while Tristan slept on the couch in the living room. I had napped for about an hour, then taken a shower and felt better than I had for days.

"Of all the people in the world, you had to reach out to...her?" Kimmie added. "She's always hated me. She blamed me for you and Chad's divorce, and every time we came here to visit, she would barely speak to me except for these harsh comments that would make me want to cry. I couldn't stand it. She always made me feel so miserable."

I sat on the bed, then found the remote and turned on the TV.

"Are you even listening?" Kimmie asked.

I looked at her. "Yes, Kimmie. I hear you. You don't like Miranda, and she doesn't like you. What do you want me to do about it? Do you have any other suggestions? If so, I'm all ears. Because I have run out of ideas and almost out of cash, I came up with this. If you have something else, then please say so."

I paused and looked at her. "No? I didn't think so."

I laid my head down on the pillow to rest, flipping through the channels. Kimmie laid next to me with a groan. We stayed like that in silence for a little while until she suddenly sat up straight.

"Why is it all my fault?"

I rolled my eyes. She really wasn't going to let this go, was she?

"What do you mean?"

"You and Miranda. You both blame me for your marriage breaking up. Has it ever occurred to you to blame Chad? He was the one who cheated. I was single at the time."

"Yeah, but you knew that he was married," I said, annoyed.

"He said you hadn't been a married couple for years—that you worked like crazy, and he never saw you. He said he tried for years to make things work, to keep the family together, but you always had something come up at work. There was always an important case pulling you away from them, making you miss birthdays and important dates, and in the end, he finally realized that it wasn't going to change. You wanted this life. He wasn't your priority. Was he lying?"

I sighed and stared at the TV. Hearing this made me feel angry and annoyed with her, even more than I already was.

"I guess he wasn't exactly lying...but..."

"I didn't think so. The way he described your marriage, I can't blame him for wanting out. You neglected your family."

I scoffed angrily.

"Hey. I was supporting my family, and yes, I was having a career. If I had been a guy, you wouldn't have thought anything of it, but because I am a woman, then it's not okay. That's just wrong. Why can't a woman have a career?"

"But you chose your work over your husband, didn't you?" she asked. "Again and again and again."

I bit my lip, knowing she was right, even though I hated to admit it. I had felt how Chad and I drifted apart but done nothing. We stopped talking, and when we did talk, we couldn't agree on anything anymore. I had kept thinking we could fix it, that there was going to be time. There was plenty of time.

Until there wasn't.

"It's none of your business," I said and grabbed the remote. I changed the channel. We weren't watching it anyway. I found an old episode of *Friends* and stopped there. "You still don't sleep with a married man. Especially not if he has children. You don't wreck a family. That's all there is to say, really. End of story."

She paused and looked at her fingers, then added. "When did you know?"

"When did I know what?"

"When did you realize that Chad was seeing someone else? That he was having an affair?"

I shrugged. "I used to say I didn't until the day he moved out, but if I'm honest, I probably knew way before then. They called once from that inn he would take you to. They left a voicemail on his cell that I accidentally heard, letting him know he had forgotten his wallet there. I know the alarms should have gone off back then, but I chose to ignore it for some reason. I think, deep down, I knew he was having an affair by then, but I just didn't want to see it. I wasn't ready. Just like I didn't want to face the fact that we had serious problems. My solution was always to work harder. There would be time to fix it later. Actually, that's how I knew where to find you at the inn. I knew it was the place he used to take you and that they took cash. Otherwise, it would have shown on our credit card statement that he had spent nights there with you and not been at conferences like he told me."

Kimmie nodded. "I see. I guess that was pretty easy then. Did I ever thank you, by the way? For saving me that day?"

"Hm, let me think; no, I don't believe you have."

Kimmie chuckled. "Okay, then. Thank you. Also, for saving me in Sykesville and taking care of Tristan and me these past several days. Without you, I would have been dead by now."

I smiled. "You're welcome."

Kimmie opened her mouth to speak, then paused as something caught her attention on the TV.

"Is that...you?"

I turned to look, then sat up straight as my picture was shown. It was an old image from my time in the FBI. I turned up the sound, my heart beating fast as the reporter told me how I was wanted by the FBI in connection with the murder of Kimmie Vanderspool, the star witness in the Wanton case.

"The suspect is considered armed and dangerous," she closed by saying.

I turned it off, heart hammering in my chest, barely able to breathe.

"Oh, no, you didn't. Isabella, tell me you didn't!"

Chapter 65

THEN:

SHE FINALLY MANAGED to get her name on TV. Samantha worked hard the next couple of months on a story that she was allowed to finish. She was standing in the newsroom when she saw her own name appear on the screen, and she shivered slightly. Samantha couldn't stop smiling as she watched her own report, seeing her hard work finally pay off. And afterward, once the anchor, Mitt Paige, had ended the broadcast and said goodnight, they all clapped for her.

"Congratulations to Samantha on her first story," the producer, Jacob, said. "That is a big deal and one heck of a story you gave us there. You have a great future ahead of you, sweetheart."

Samantha blushed at his kind words before she went to her desk to grab her purse and go home for the night. She was shutting down her computer first, and that's when a colleague, Jeremy, came over to her.

"Hey, congrats on your big story."

"Thanks," she said with a wide smile. She couldn't help herself; she simply couldn't stop.

"Say, we need to celebrate, right?"

Samantha looked at her watch. It was getting late. She already had her eyes on a new story she wanted to start the next day, covering a scandal at the local university, and she had the first research interview set up in the morning.

"I really need to..."

"A group of us is going to Mitt Paige's apartment after this to hang out and have a few beers. You should come."

"To Mitt Paige's apartment?"

"Yeah. A bunch of us are going. We would go out to a bar or something, but Mitt hates those places since people always come up to him and talk to him, feeling like they know him, and then he feels like he has to talk to them all night instead of relaxing. It's the life of a celebrity. So, that's why he has asked us all to come to his place instead."

Samantha stared at Jeremy. He was about twice her age. She knew he was married and had children, and he seemed to care much for his family. She had seen his pictures of them on his screensaver on his laptop, and she had heard him talk more than once about his twins and the crazy things they did with great affection in his voice and eyes. He didn't seem to be flirting with her, and she felt safe in his presence. She did want to celebrate her accomplishment, and she had never really hung out with any of the anchors. Going to his apartment was quite a big deal. It wasn't something everyone was invited to.

You need to live a little. It can't be all work and no play.

Jeremy smiled and grabbed his jacket from behind his chair. "You coming? We can share a cab."

Samantha looked at her phone. Natasha was calling her, probably to congratulate her. She stared at her name, then decided not to pick it up. Instead, she looked up at Jeremy and put the ringing phone into her purse.

"I guess I could go for just one beer."

Chapter 66

"You do realize your face is all over the news, right?"

I kicked a rock on the road. I had walked down the street from the farm and then continued for like half an hour to make sure my phone call wasn't traced to Miranda's farm. Just in case. I couldn't be too careful, even though I was using another burner phone.

"You're wanted in connection with murder?" my dad chuckled. "What the heck have you been up to this time?"

"I'm too exhausted even to explain," I said.

He grew silent. "Please, tell me you're being careful, kid."

"I'm doing my best."

"I might have the info you needed," he said.

"I love how fast you are. What have you got?"

"John Savage, news director of WBC News, right hand to Richard Wanton, CEO of WBC News. Those two have been friends since college and have been helping each other out. When Wanton got promoted, Savage followed him up the ladder and took his former position."

"And was he questioned in connection with the investigation of Wanton?"

"Yes. Several times."

"Really?"

"He had an alibi for the night, but not a very tight one. His wife said they were together all night and that they went to bed around midnight."

"Were there any indications that he might have been in the apartment?"

"They found his fingerprints there, but it was easily explained by him often coming there, and he had been there earlier the same day when the two of them had a meeting in Wanton's office. A lady who cleans for Wanton testified to seeing him arrive around two o'clock and leave at five, leaving behind empty glasses of scotch. At six-thirty, Wanton left to go to dinner, according to the doorman."

"Where he met with Kimmie. And Samantha Durkin? When did she get there?"

"She arrived at eight-thirty that night and was let in by the doorman who had seen her with Wanton before and believed her when she said she was meeting Wanton at his apartment. Wanton says he barely knew her and that she was obsessed with him, and that she was stalking him. He stated that he hadn't asked her to come, that she had come on her own, and it was as much a surprise to him that she was there inside his apartment as it was to Kimmie."

I wrinkled my forehead. "Really? That's his excuse? What a poor one. No one will ever believe that."

"That was his statement over and over again, according to the report."

"I see."

"And Savage's role in all this?" my dad asked.

"That's what I'm trying to figure out. I have a feeling he was also there on that night, but I just can't figure out how he fits in."

"They have been known to cover for each other," my dad said. "These guys will do anything for one another. Maybe Wanton is taking the fall for him?"

"But why would he do that?"

"Because he owes him?"

I nodded, biting my lip. It was plausible but just didn't ring right with me.

"Whatever it is, Eva Rae," my dad said, "promise me you'll be careful. These are powerful people. They'll do anything to protect themselves and each other. Anything."

Chapter 67

They were shown into John Savage's office by his assistant, and the door closed behind them. Rachel felt her hands get clammy as she threw a glance around the room. The interior was decorated very modernly, with a glass desk in the center and big windows behind it, showing the view over the yard and trees behind the white modern architectural designed house. It had a lot of sleek and clean surfaces, and Rachel didn't see any dust on any of the shelves. The huge Mac computer screen on the glass desk seemed brand-new.

"Sorry if I'm late," a voice said behind her as the door opened and a man stepped inside. Rachel held her breath as she recognized John Savage. He had a serious look on his face. And he wasn't alone. Behind him came two suit-wearing men, carrying briefcases. Seeing them made Rachel's heart drop.

"I thought I was just going to talk to him?" she whispered to Crystal.

Rachel stared at the men, heart hammering in her chest. Did they expect her to tell her story to all these people? Just like that? She had never talked to any of them before, and they were men. Her story was quite private and personal, and she wasn't sure she would be able to.

"Crystal?"

"Let's sit down," Crystal said and pointed at the conference table. Rachel followed her and grabbed a chair, then sat down. The men sat across from them. None of them seemed to look directly at her, and that made her feel uncomfortable.

"We've read your statement, Rachel McBeal," one of them said, looking down at his papers and not up at her. He had short red hair and freckles covering his face. He seemed young.

"What do you mean?" she asked, puzzled. "I didn't give any statement."

He pushed a piece of paper across the table toward her, and she looked at it, then up at Crystal.

"But that was...that was just for you. I wrote my story for you to read, not for anyone else to see. I wrote it because it was hard for me to say it out loud. It wasn't supposed to be seen by anyone else or used for... What's going on here?"

Crystal wasn't looking at her either. Rachel felt like her throat was getting tighter. She had to take a couple of deep breaths to calm herself. Her heart was pounding loudly.

"How did this man get the...excuse me, who are you people?" Rachel said.

"We are Lipman and Nichols, Attorneys at Law, representing our client, Richard Wanton."

"Wanton? But..." she turned to look at Crystal. "What is this? Did you know they'd be here? I...I don't understand."

"It has come to our attention that you are making some pretty serious accusations against our client," the redhead said. "We're here to make sure you stop doing that."

Rachel almost dropped her jaw. "Excuse me? What do you mean?"

"In this statement, you are accusing our client of rape, am I correct?"

Rachel felt confused. She kept looking at Crystal for help, but she didn't say a word. "I have just told my story, but this was private..."

"We need you to stop doing that. It is a lie from one end to the other."

Rachel's eyes grew wide. Her heart was hammering so hard in her chest, it almost hurt. She felt dizzy, unable to focus properly. It felt like a nightmare.

"What...who...?"

"We have here a contract that we want you to sign today. By doing so, you agree not to accuse our client of rape again."

"I'm not gonna...no...why...?"

The redhead tilted his head.

"Just sign it, please."

"No. I have the right to tell my story. You can't take that away from me. He hurt me, and I am going to say that once we take this to court."

"You're on Prozac, right? We have here a picture of the prescription medicine, and your name clearly stated on the bottle."

He pushed the picture toward her so she could see it.

"How did you get that?"

"You're not reliable," he continued. "In fact, you're mentally unstable. No one will believe you. You have a mental disorder. You suffer from anxiety, am I right?"

"I...I had a panic attack because..."

The redhead interrupted her. "How can you claim to be a sane person? How do you expect a judge to believe your story? It won't stand up in court."

Rachel's shoulders tensed. She didn't understand anything. What was going on here?

"But...I'm...not..."

"And you drink too, am I right?" he said and pulled out a picture. He turned it to show her. "That is you, right? Behind all those empty bottles? This is a picture of you we're looking at, right? Drinking with your friends?"

"But...that picture..." she turned to look at Crystal. "You took that. On the day we were out eating. You ordered all those bottles of wine, not me. And now it makes it look like I was drinking all that?"

Crystal didn't say anything. She fiddled with her papers, looking down.

Rachel scoffed, her shoulders coming down.

"You're working for them. You've been working for them all this time, haven't you? You took the picture of my prescription medicine on the day you visited me at my house? You found it in my bathroom. You were never on my side, were you? You were never going to help us—any of us. You were sent out to track all the women down that might have a story on Wanton to make sure we're found and forced to shut up. Because of the trial. Wow. How could I have been so stupid? How could I have...you tricked me?"

Rachel rose to her feet, pushing the chair back with a swift movement that almost tipped it over.

"I need to go."

She grabbed her purse and bag, then rushed toward the door, heart pounding in her chest, trying to avoid the panic from settling in.

"No one will ever believe you, Rachel," the redhead yelled after her. "You're mentally unstable and a drunk."

Crying heavily, her entire body shaking in panic and anxiety, Rachel opened the door, then ran out into the hallway and down the stairs, while she could still hear the lawyer's words ringing in her head.

Mentally unstable. A drunk. That's all you are, Rachel. That's all you are.

As she stormed for the front door, she passed a woman standing in the hallway, big sad eyes lingering on her. She looked fragile and small and like she wanted to say something to Rachel. She reached out her hand toward her, but Rachel pulled away, crying, then ran out the front door.

Chapter 68

"I don't get it," I said and slammed the door shut behind me. I had walked back to the farmhouse where Kimmie was sitting in the kitchen with a warm cup of coffee between her hands.

She looked up, a little startled.

"What was John's role in all this?"

She shook her head. "I told you to let it go. He wasn't there. He's Wanton's best friend, yes, but he wasn't at the apartment. You heard me wrong."

I stared at her, feeling how annoyed I was, trying not to let it get to me. Everything about this woman made me so frustrated.

"I don't think you've told me the truth," I said. "You're hiding something, something important."

Kimmie gave me an annoyed look. "Why won't you let it go? I told you what happened in the apartment. End of story."

I exhaled. "I'm not so sure you have. At least not all of it. I know when I'm being lied to, Kimmie."

She tilted her head. "Really? Chad lied to you for more than a year, and you didn't notice."

I stared down at her, my nostrils flaring, fighting to control myself. I grabbed my laptop, then walked toward the bedroom. Before walking in there, I turned to look at her:

"Maybe I did notice. Maybe I even knew. Maybe I just decided not to care."

She didn't say anything, and I walked into the bedroom and closed the door behind me. I felt like running back out there and strangling her but kept myself as calm as possible. I stayed in the room for hours as it grew dark outside. When Miranda came in and said there was food, I told her I wasn't hungry. I had things to do, thoughts to conquer. I couldn't grasp this story. I couldn't wrap my head around it, and my intuition told me something was completely off. It all boiled down to the motive. Why would Wanton kill Samantha Durkin? Had she threatened him? Was he scared she might expose him? But then why do it there? Why did he do it in his own apartment? Because he got so mad at her? Because he reacted in anger? It didn't seem like him to be so irrational. He was a calculated man, someone who had played the game to get to the top. What could make him lose it like that?

I sat on the floor of my bedroom until bedtime, wondering about these things, when Miranda knocked on the door and came inside.

"There's someone on the phone for you, on my cell. I tried to tell him you weren't here, but he wouldn't listen to me. He said he knew you were and that he's your...dad? I thought I knew your dad?"

I stared up at her. "It's a long story. I'll tell it to you later."

I grabbed her cell in my hand. "What are you doing calling me here? What if they track your phone? And how the heck did you know where to find me? I didn't tell you where I am."

My dad cleared his throat. "Do you really want to know all that, or just know that I am good at finding people and trust that I know how to protect myself from being traced, as I am...a pretty skilled hacker?"

"Okay, point taken, and no, I probably don't want to know more. Why are you calling me?"

"I got something for you, something you'll really like."

"Really?"

"Oh, yeah. I couldn't help myself after talking to you. I needed to know more. So, I gained access to John Savage's private computer and snooped around for quite a while. You wouldn't believe what I found."

Chapter 69

THEN:

THEY SHARED A CAB THERE. Samantha got out and walked up to the building, following Jeremy. He pressed a button at the intercom, then received an answer, and the door was buzzed open. Jeremy held the door for Samantha. She walked up the stairs, and he came up behind her.

"It's on the third floor, on your right."

It wasn't where Mitt Paige lived with his family, Samantha had been told. This was a place he slept when working because he lived almost two hours outside of D.C with his wife and son. And when he often had late shifts or early ones, he'd stay the night in the apartment, so he didn't need to commute the next day. It was something several of the anchors did.

"Just walk straight in," Jeremy said as Samantha approached the door. She felt a little shy just to walk into his place like that but did it anyway. Inside, there was music blasting from the living room, and she followed it until she stood inside and didn't see anyone else.

She turned to look at Jeremy, who walked past her. Mitt Paige came out of the kitchen, holding three beers, then handed her one.

"Wh-where is everyone else?" she asked nervously.

Mitt Paige smiled the way he was known for on TV. "They couldn't make it. It's okay. We're celebrating you today. Cheers."

He clinked his bottle against hers, and Samantha felt herself calm down, then drank. Mitt was such a nice guy. He was everyone's TV darling but was actually really nice in real life too. And funny. They sat down on a bench at the small dining table. Jeremy sat on the chair across from them with a deep, satisfied exhale.

"It was a good show tonight. I think we can be really satisfied with that one."

"Your story was amazing, Sam," Mitt said. "Congratulations on that one."

"Yeah, that is a big deal," Jeremy said. "I remember my first story. Oh, boy, that is what...? Fifteen, no seventeen years ago. Oh, my, we're getting old, Mitt."

"Speak for yourself. I'm still young and handsome," Mitt said with a deep laugh.

Jeremy leaned forward. "I remember my intern days. Mitt and I were in the same place; you remember that, Mitt?"

"How could I forget. You stole my story. Don't you ever let this guy know of anything you're working on," Mitt said and drank again. "He'll steal it and make it his own. And then you're stuck being an anchor for the rest of your life because no one thinks you can actually do anything else. Reduced to being nothing but a pretty face."

"Yeah, right. We feel really sorry for you, Mitt," Jeremy said, laughing. "Oh...Do you remember that old producer we had?"

"The guy who was senile, but no one wanted to admit it? He couldn't remember which story he had given to who or what day it was, but everyone covered for him because he was so loved, so somehow, he always managed to pull together a decent news broadcast. What was his name again?"

"Kurt something," Jeremy said and finished his beer.

Sam took another sip and looked at the two men. She truly enjoyed hearing these old stories from back in the day. It was one of the things she loved about the media business. So many funny characters, and it was never boring. People were so interesting and had tried so much in their lives. Even though she had felt a little uneasy at being alone with these two men, she felt suddenly very comfortable. They were like uncles to her, telling her stories from their youth. It was really sweet.

"We can do another round, right?" Mitt said and got up. He walked to the kitchen before Sam could protest and tell him that she hadn't even finished the first one, and she probably had to go home now.

He came back a few seconds later, carrying three more beers, then handed one to Jeremy and left the other two on the round table. Then he sat down on the other side of where he had been sitting earlier, very close to Samantha.

Part V

THE TRIAL

Chapter 70

On the day the trial started, I traveled to D.C. with Kimmie and Tristan sitting in the back, me in the front, while Miranda drove the old purple Chevrolet pick-up truck. No one said a word. I guess we were all too nervous. And to be honest, I had no idea how this was ever going to end well.

"So, what's the plan here?" Miranda finally said as we reached the sign telling us we were fifteen miles outside of D.C. "I know you haven't told me much about what this is or what is going to happen, but someone's gotta ask, right?"

I stared at her, then out the window at the landscape rushing by. I didn't know what to say. Miranda took the exit, and we drove toward downtown. That's when I spotted the black sedan in the side-view mirror. I kept an eye on it for a little while until I felt certain it was following us.

"Say, that black sedan has been on our tail for the past ten minutes," I said, addressed to Miranda. "Have you noticed that?"

Miranda looked in the rearview mirror with a "huh."

I glared at it in the mirror, my pulse quickening. Miranda slowed down at a red light. The sedan drove up on our side and came closer.

As it did, I saw the driver lift a gun inside the cabin. I acted quickly, turned to face Kimmie and Tristan, and yelled:

"GET DOWN!"

They both threw themselves forward toward the floor, and I bent down, covering my head while the shots rained on our truck. We all screamed, and Miranda stepped on the accelerator and jerked the wheel to the left. The truck took a sharp turn before hitting the car in front of us. Miranda then steered it onto the street ahead and took a turn down a smaller road, almost hitting the oncoming traffic as she did. Cars were honking at us while Miranda very skillfully steered us down the one-way street, avoiding ramming into the cars coming toward us, sometimes by barely an inch. Inside the cabin, we were thrown around as she tried to lose the black sedan that was pursuing us, refusing to let us get away.

"Hold on tight," Miranda screamed at the top of her lungs as she took a sharp turn right, and the truck skidded sideways on the asphalt, then jolted forward again.

"WATCH OUT!" I screamed as I stared directly into the front grill of a huge delivery truck.

Miranda pulled the wheel hard to the right again and steered clear of the truck as it blasted past us, blowing its deep horn.

Gasping for air, I looked in the mirror and saw the sedan pull up behind us, coming closer rapidly.

"They're still on our tail."

"How far to the courthouse?"

"Two more blocks," I said.

Miranda nodded. "All right. Hold on tight."

She took a turn left, then one right, zigzagging through traffic, the sedan keeping up right behind us. Then, as she took a turn down one street, the traffic closed up in front of us, and we were stuck.

The sedan came up behind us, then drove up on our side again.

"Get down in the back," I said to Kimmie and Tristan.

"I've just about had it with these people," Miranda said as she leaned over me and pulled something out from behind the back of my seat.

A shotgun.

She cocked it, then asked me to lean back, placed it out the window, and fired at the sedan. The shot shattered their window. Traffic was moving again ahead of us, and Miranda cocked the gun again, then handed it to me.

"Take out their tires."

I stared at her. She got impatient and yelled:

"Are you waiting for me to ask politely?"

I shook my head, then did as she said. I aimed at a tire and fired. The front tire exploded while Miranda stepped on the accelerator and floored it, tires screeching. The truck jolted forward, and she zigzagged between cars while I stared at the sedan that remained in place behind us.

Chapter 71

As expected, the place was crawling with journalists, cameras flickering, and reporters doing lives from the stairs outside the courthouse. Rachel smiled at the sight, remembering her own days as a reporter, waiting for endless hours for a verdict in a high-profile case. She didn't think she would, but she realized she actually missed it.

She walked up the stairs, then past the heavy security and police guarding the doors. She went through the security check and then continued toward the courtroom. As she entered, she had to take a deep breath. In the front, the first thing she saw was Richard Wanton, sitting at the desk with his team of high-profile lawyers. Behind him, she spotted Wanton's wife and his best friend John Savage, sitting close to his wife, Carol. Rachel felt sick to her stomach thinking about the last time she had seen John Savage at his house.

The bastard.

On the other side, she spotted FBI director Isabella Horne, recognizing her from TV, along with her colleagues and what she assumed was the prosecutor. They wore serious expressions and seemed nervous. According to the news this morning, they had reason to be.

They didn't have much evidence, and it was anticipated that the case would be dismissed.

"All rise for the Honorable Judge Moore," a voice yelled, and they stood to their feet as the judge came in. He sat down, then looked seriously at all of them. "Counselors, please approach the bench."

He spoke with a low voice to them, then looked at the prosecutor and said loudly: "Do you or don't you have a witness?"

Just as he said the words, Carol Savage turned her head and met Rachel's gaze in the back of the courtroom.

As their eyes met, they both smiled.

Chapter 72

THEN:

IT ALL WENT DOWN SO FAST; she barely had time to react. Sitting next to her, very close, Mitt stared at Samantha intensely. There had been a shift in his eyes—in the way he looked at her, and it immediately made her uneasy.

The corners of his lips twisted into a smirk right before he lifted his hand and placed it on top of her mouth. Then, using his weight, he pressed her down onto the bench she was sitting on.

Confused, Samantha didn't know what to think. Mitt's hands were on her face, pressing her down while he laid on top of her, his fingers piercing into her skin as she tried to move beneath him. All she could think about for some reason was Jeremy. She couldn't lift her head to look because Mitt was holding her head down, and every time she tried to, he pushed her back down, using his weight. But for some reason, it was all she could think about—Jeremy and whether or not he was still sitting there. Was he watching what was happening? For reasons she couldn't understand, she worried that he was because she believed it was the most embarrassing thing in the world if he were still there.

Why isn't Mitt kissing me if he likes me?

Samantha squirmed beneath his weight while Mitt pulled up her skirt and penetrated her, still holding her down, pressing his hands on her mouth. The bench was hard on her back and uncomfortable, and she felt a pain stab her. She wanted to say something; she wanted to scream and kick him off, but somehow, she couldn't. Instead, she froze completely. It was like every part of her body became immobilized, and she gave up the fight.

She let him have his way.

At some point, she managed to lift her head just enough to peek above the table, and that's when she realized that Jeremy had gone. He was no longer sitting there, which gave her profound relief. Maybe he hadn't seen anything after all? Yet, she suddenly couldn't stop wondering why he had just left. If he had seen Mitt press her onto the bench, why didn't he say something? Why didn't he stop him?

As she was thinking this, Mitt lifted his hand and slapped her across the face, and she fell back onto the bench, her cheek burning while Mitt placed an elbow on her face to keep her down. Samantha focused on lying completely still, hoping it would be over soon, trying to think as little as possible.

When he was done, Mitt sat up on the bench, pulled out a cigarette, and then lit it. Samantha sat up next to him, still feeling confused, asking herself what had just happened.

He handed her a cigarette. "Smoke?"

She shook her head.

He put the pack away, then inhaled and exhaled with a satisfied grunt. Then, he looked at her.

"I like the way that I just took you. Just like that."

He snapped his fingers with a grin. Samantha forced a smile, not quite knowing what to say. She stared at him, unable to figure out how to react.

He grinned at her again. "I would like to do other stuff with you."

Samantha grabbed her purse.

"I...I should go home."

He rose to his feet and approached her. "There's something my wife won't do with me. I'd like to try that with you."

He placed a hand on her shoulder, and it felt so heavy that Samantha slumped forward. She avoided looking into his eyes. Instead, she just said goodbye, then rushed out of the apartment and into the rainy street, feeling how everyone's eyes lingered on her, how they could all see, just by looking at her, what she had done.

Chapter 73

"Director Horne?"

Isabella Horne looked up at Judge Moore.

"Can you possibly shed some light onto this mystery?" he asked. "I am very close to dismissing your case because the way I see it, you really don't have enough for us to continue. If you can't bring more to the table, I have no other option than to declare Richard Wanton free of all charges."

A murmur rushed through the crowd.

Isabella Horne cleared her throat. "Your Honor, I..."

"I don't want to hear any more excuses, Director. Do you have a witness or not?"

Silence spread inside the courtroom. Everyone was holding their breath, waiting to hear the outcome.

"I might be able to answer that question, Your Honor."

I stepped inside the courtroom, and all eyes turned to look at us. Kimmie was right behind me, while Miranda had taken Tristan with her to a seat among the spectators. I walked closer.

"I believe I have the witness Director Horne is missing," I said.

Isabella stared at me, eyes wide.

"Eva Rae Thomas?"

I approached her. "Yes, surprisingly alive and well. And so is Kimmie here. Ready to testify to what happened on the night Samantha Durkin died."

"Eva Rae...I..." Isabella started.

"This woman is wanted for murder," my former FBI colleague Timmy Gardner yelled, standing up from his seat. He sat back down when Isabella gave him a look.

Isabella faced me. "Eva Rae...You..."

I stopped her. "Save it for later. I know you didn't send those people to kill me. I know you weren't the leak. Timmy was."

I turned to face Timmy Gardner in his seat. The big guy squirmed. "I found the video Savage used to blackmail you into giving him the information on where the FBI kept Kimmie and what she told us. That girl in the video is a minor. No wonder your wife divorced you." I turned to look at Isabella. "My guess is he also deleted the surveillance footage, but you'll have to talk to him about that. I'll send you everything later. Then, you can deal with him."

Judge Moore slammed his gavel. "Could we please get some order in the courtroom? Now, will anyone explain to me what is going on? Please, approach the bench."

Isabella grabbed my hand and pulled me with her toward the judge. Kimmie came up behind us.

"All right. Could someone please clarify for me what on earth is going on here? Do you have a witness or not?"

"We do, Your Honor," Isabella said and pulled Kimmie closer. "This woman was in the apartment when Samantha Durkin fell to her death from the terrace. She saw what happened and has agreed to testify."

I bit my lip, hesitating for just a second, then said:

"But I am afraid her testimony won't be what we expected it to be."

A gasp went through the crowd, and the judge slammed his gavel again. "Order, order!"

He looked down at me. "Now, what is that supposed to mean?"

I exhaled. "That the statement that the witness gave to the FBI during the interrogation was a complete and utter lie."

Chapter 74

THEN:

"You need to get up."

Natasha stood at the end of Samantha's bed, then turned on the lights. "You've been lying here for days now."

Samantha pulled the covers over her head. Nat pulled them back down, so she could look at her.

"What's going on with you? I don't think you're sick."

"Just let me sleep."

"You haven't been to work in forever; that's not like you. Sam, you love your job. What's going on with you?"

Samantha exhaled. "I called in sick. I'm just tired; that's all."

"I'm not buying that," Nat said. "Please, talk to me. Something happened, something bad. And don't tell me I'm wrong. I know you."

Samantha looked at her friend. She wanted to tell her to leave, to yell something awful at her so she would never come back. The last thing she wanted at this moment was for her good friend to look at her with judgmental eyes and tell her how big a mess she had made of her life.

Yet, for some reason, she did it anyway. She felt the urge to talk about what had happened, even though she was terrified of what Nat would say to it, how she would tell her she was a disgusting whore. Because that's how she felt. So dirty.

Such a mess.

"Something did happen," Sam said. "But I don't know how to tell you. I am so embarrassed."

Nat placed a hand on her shoulder, then smiled. "Try anyway."

Samantha swallowed hard, then looked down at her fingers. She then told her the story of what had happened at Mitt Paige's apartment, but she left out the names, so Nat wouldn't know who it was.

As she was done, she looked up at her friend, terrified when seeing the look on her face.

"Oh, God, I never should have told you," she said and hid her face between her hands. "You hate me now."

Nat grabbed her wrists, pulled her hands away from her face, and then forced her to look into her eyes.

"Sweetie, look at me. The guy, this man, whoever he was, he...he raped you."

Samantha stared at Nat, heart knocking hard in her chest, then shook her head. "No...no, you don't understand. I went up to the apartment willingly. I didn't scream or kick or fight him. I think...I led him to believe he was allowed to do it. I must have said something; if only I could figure out what it was that I said, or did, to make him believe that's what I wanted. That I liked it."

"First of all, I don't believe that about you. But it doesn't matter. You're not allowed to do that to a woman, to put a hand on top of her mouth and press her down like that. That's not okay. No matter what she said or did."

Samantha was breathing heavily now, tears pressing behind her eyes. "But...he was so nice? Afterward, he was kind, and...maybe he thought I liked it."

"Makes no difference, Sam. And you know it. Deep down in your heart, you know this. You think he was somehow entitled to do this to you, just to take you as he said afterward. You think you somehow gave him permission."

"Well, maybe he thought that because...because he heard I was with Wanton, then..."

"Then he was allowed to do this to you? No way. It wouldn't matter if you slept with a hundred men at the station. It doesn't justify what he did to you."

Tears welled up in Sam's eyes, and some of them escaped, then rolled down her cheeks. She didn't bother wiping them away.

"But I am a whore. That's who I am. And they all know it."

Nat grabbed Sam and pulled her into a deep hug. "Oh, sweet girl. Don't you ever think that about yourself. These men abused you. You need to fight back. Go to HR, do you hear me? Tell your story, then let them be the judge of whether or not what happened is wrong. Don't let them get away with this, you hear me? They had no right to treat you like this. None whatsoever."

Chapter 75

"I will not have this disruption again, or I will clear the courtroom."

A loud burst of murmurs and shocked gasps had broken out among the spectators, and the judge tried once again to calm them. Finally, the room went quiet, and all eyes were on me.

"Continue," Judge Moore said.

I cleared my throat.

"What do you mean it is a lie?" Isabella said. "I heard her testify on the recordings, telling you that Wanton pushed Samantha Durkin."

I turned to look at Kimmie. She looked beyond terrified. I hadn't told her that I knew because I feared she wouldn't show up in the courtroom if I did. I was determined to get the truth out, no matter what the outcome was going to be.

"Do you want to tell them, or should I?"

She was shaking heavily, her eyes growing wide. "I...I don't..."

I placed a hand on her shoulder. "I know, Kimmie. I know what you were up to. I have the video from Wanton's apartment. It was on John Savage's computer, along with the video of Timmy and that girl. It wasn't hard to connect the dots from there."

You could cut through the silence in the room as everyone waited for Kimmie to open up and explain. She stared at me, her lips vibrating, but no words left her mouth.

"There is a video?" Judge Moore asked. "Why haven't I been informed of this?"

"I didn't know either," Isabella said. "Eva Rae, what is this video, and where did it come from? Who recorded a video?"

I was still looking at Kimmie, waiting for her to reply, but when she didn't, I took over. "My guess is Kimmie did."

"What?" Isabella said. "I don't understand."

"It was recorded with a phone from inside the apartment, from the living room while Samantha and Richard Wanton were on the rooftop deck, talking. You see them arguing loudly, and that all fits with Kimmie's story, but then you see Samantha come back to Kimmie, and you hear her say something that isn't exactly what Kimmie told us. What did she say, Kimmie?"

Kimmie was biting her lip, then looked down at her fingers.

"Miss Vanderspool," Judge Moore said. "Just tell us. We will see the video later anyway."

Kimmie nodded. I could tell she was about to cry, but she was fighting it.

"I...she...Samantha told me that it wasn't going the way she wanted it to."

"And what did she mean by that?" I asked.

"I don't know."

"Yes, you do. Come on, Kimmie. You planned this night, didn't you? You and Samantha. You deliberately ran into Wanton the week before and made him believe you'd do anything for a job. You knew he'd try to get you into his bed. It's how he operated. Then, when he suggested it after dinner, you went with him, knowing that Samantha would be in the apartment because you and she had made sure she would sneak in while you were having dinner with Wanton. Samantha bribed the doorman to let her in, then got ready for you both to get there. Wanton was surprised to see her; you conveniently forgot to mention that during the interview. You and Samantha wanted to film him asking for sex in exchange for a job, am I right? And if that didn't work, then Samantha would sleep with him, and you could film him, and he'd get in trouble for having sex with an intern, which is against company policy. You wanted him to get fired. That's how you'd get back at him for how he had treated both of you. Am I wrong?"

Chapter 76

THEN:

"Go ahead, Miss Durkin," the secretary sitting outside the wooden doors said. "Mr. Wanton can see you now."

Samantha rose to her feet, her pulse quickening. She walked to the door, then took a couple of deep breaths, trying to calm herself as she pushed it open.

Richard Wanton was standing behind his desk as she entered. He barely looked up. "Ah, Miss Durkin. Come on in."

Samantha closed the door behind her, then approached his desk.

"Sit down, please," he said, signing something, then pushing it aside. They both sat down. He finally looked at her, then exhaled, satisfied. He spoke in almost a whisper:

"It's good to see you again."

She smiled shyly. "I'm here because..."

"Ah, yes, HR sent over the papers," he said and grabbed a file on his desk. He flipped through it carelessly. Wanton leaned back in his leather chair, folding his hands on his chest, his eyes scrutinizing her.

"Mitt Paige, huh?"

Samantha nodded. She had a lump in her throat that threatened to explode. Wanton smiled.

"You've been busy since you got here, haven't you?"

She looked up, and her eyes met his. "What do you mean by…?"

"I mean, you've been busy. You want me to believe Mitt Paige actually raped you? You went up into his apartment, Samantha. What did you expect would happen?"

"I…I…he pressed me down; he held me down…"

"Yes, I have read the report, and frankly, I don't believe a word of it. I have known Paige for years. He's my star, the network's superstar. I'm not gonna let you come here and ruin everything with your stories. I know who you are. You came to my hotel room, remember? Are you gonna accuse me of raping you too?"

Samantha looked down, tears piling up in her eyes.

"I…I'm pregnant."

"Oh, wow, that's just great, isn't it?" he said, throwing out his hands. "It's Mitt's, of course. And now you're threatening to tell the world that our beloved anchor is a rapist and the father of your child. But I tell you what. You get rid of that child, you hear me? You get an abortion, and you never tell anyone that story you're making up here. No one is going to believe you, Sam. It's not like you've been a nun around here. I mean, you kept running after me, wanting to meet up in restrooms and calling me late at night. You've been stalking me, and I almost reported you. I don't believe your story, and neither will anyone else. You're nothing but a worthless whore, and you'll never work in this business again. Now, leave before I have you thrown out of my TV station."

Crying, Samantha sprang to her feet and ran out of the office. She went into the elevator and tried to control her sobs, cursing Nat far away for pressuring her to do this when she knew it wouldn't end well—when she knew she herself was to blame for what happened.

Just as the doors were about to close, someone arrived and put their hand in the door. They opened again, and a woman stepped inside.

"Phew, I barely made it."

She got in and stood next to Samantha as the doors finally closed. When the elevator began to move, Sam could no longer keep her crying at bay, and she burst into tears. The woman grabbed her and hugged her.

"Oh, dear Lord. Is it that bad? Tell me everything, dear child. Everything."

Chapter 77

"Wanton wanted Sam to cover up the fact that his star anchor, Mitt Paige, had raped Samantha," Kimmie said. "He forced her to get an abortion and threatened her to silence. Samantha got the abortion, but she was so miserable she could barely get by. So, we started to plan this, yes. We wanted to get back at him, to take him down, hopefully get him fired for how he was treating women."

"But it didn't go as planned. That's what Samantha said when coming to you in the living room where you were filming," I said. "Then, what happened?"

Kimmie exhaled. "I...she said she wasn't sure she'd be able to get him to try and have sex with her. He was angry and wanted her to leave. Then, she said she had another plan. We hadn't discussed this, so it took me completely by surprise."

"What did she say to you?" I asked.

"She said, 'whatever happens, just go along with it.' Then, I asked her what she planned to do. She said she had seen a police car below, parking on the street. When the officers came back out, she'd do it. 'They'll think he killed me. If you testify that he did kill me, he'll go down.'"

"She wanted to frame him for murder?" I asked.

Kimmie nodded. "I wasn't prepared for it. I...I just stared at her, then said I thought we should leave."

"And at this point, you're still filming, right?"

"Yes, the phone is in my lap, so you can't see anything, but you can hear our conversation."

"And then what happened?"

Kimmie swallowed. She glanced up at the judge briefly, then lowered her eyes again. "Then she went back out there. And..."

"And what, Kimmie? What did she do?"

Kimmie exhaled. "She...jumped."

I closed my eyes as another gasp went through the crowd.

"Now, you don't see that in the video, do you?" I asked.

Kimmie shook her head. "No."

"As I said, I watched it, and you don't. But you do hear you scream, and go, 'no, Samantha, no!'"

Kimmie nodded. Tears were in her eyes as she looked up at me.

"She was just...gone."

"And then your troubles began," I said. "You wanted to honor her last wish and blame it all on Wanton. That way, you'd also get what you came for, which was revenge on him for what he did to you back in the day, but that meant you had to lie to the FBI and later in court."

"I thought it would be easier if I said it in front of you," she said.

"Well, you had a history of lying to me already, throughout an entire year when you slept with my husband."

Kimmie looked down, then nodded.

"What did he do to you?" I asked. "What did Wanton do to you?"

She looked up. "He got me pregnant, then told me I had to get rid of it if I ever wanted to work in the media industry again."

"But you didn't. You kept the child. Tristan is his?"

Kimmie nodded. "And I never could get a decent job again. But it was worth it because I love my son."

I smiled, thinking for the first time that I had gained respect for

Kimmie. Everything else she did, I couldn't agree with, but sacrificing everything for your son—that I could get on board with. That, I could respect.

"I told you I was innocent! You wouldn't believe me. I didn't murder that woman!"

I turned to look at Richard Wanton, who had risen from his seat. His eyes were gleaming with victory.

"You all heard what she said," he continued. "You are my witnesses. Samantha jumped. She was nothing but a crazy stalker, just like I said she was. And I am an innocent man."

Chapter 78

"Not so fast," I said and looked at Wanton. "We're not completely done here. There are a few things that haven't been clarified. Like what was the video doing on John Savage's computer?"

Wanton looked at me, puzzled. "I don't care how it got there."

"Well, I do," I said and took a step toward him. "I don't like loose ends. They keep me awake at night. And they did all last night. I couldn't stop wondering about that and the fact that Kimmie, in her statement, said she ran to the bedroom to grab her purse and look for her phone to call for help. Why was she looking for her phone if she was recording with it in the living room?"

Wanton scoffed mockingly. "Who cares?"

"I do, Mr. Wanton," Judge Moore said. "Continue, Mrs. Thomas."

"It drove me nuts. Why was Kimmie searching frantically for her phone? Did she lie about that? But it would be a strange thing to lie about, I thought. There was no reason for it. It wouldn't be odd if she had her phone close to her when sitting in the living room. Why tell a lie? Because it wasn't a lie. It was the truth. Because the phone

Kimmie was using to record what was supposed to be a sex scene wasn't hers. It was someone else's, someone who wasn't present in the apartment. That's why she answered weirdly when I kept asking if someone else was there. Because this person wasn't there, but their phone was. But no one could know that, so Kimmie couldn't use that phone to call nine-one-one. Otherwise, she risked placing this other person in correlation with Sam's death. They would be asked about it, maybe even implicated. They couldn't risk that since this person was the one who had made sure they met one another. This person was the one who had helped them birth this plan to get Wanton."

"And so, who is this third person?" Judge Moore asked.

"I wondered for a long time about that. Kimmie had insinuated to me that someone else was involved, that there had been three of them. And then she over spoke one day, saying the name John. So naturally, I assumed it was John Savage, but it made no sense that he would be helping them. He was Wanton's best friend through so many years and his right hand. It wasn't until last night when I realized that Kimmie hadn't finished the sentence. She was about to say something else when she stopped herself. She was about to say John's *wife*. That's when I realized that my hacker who provided me with this material had gained access to the family cloud, not just John Savage's computer. It was John's wife who was behind it. Carol Savage. She was also the woman who met Samantha in the elevator. Am I right, Carol?"

I turned to look at the woman sitting next to John Savage on the bench. Her eyes gleamed at me, and then she smiled.

Chapter 79

Rachel watched with bated breath as Carol rose to her feet in front of the room. She had been watching this scene unfold from the back, and now she felt like screaming at Carol.

Don't do it! Don't reveal yourself!

Rachel had met with Carol soon after the day in her home when her husband had tried to intimidate her into silence. She had assured her that she could help her, that the battle wasn't lost yet. Then, she had introduced her to several other girls, all with stories similar to hers. Some of them were the very same that she had met with the fake woman Crystal, who had turned out to be working for Wanton. But Carol had gathered them all and assured her that the battle had just begun. She had also asked Rachel to show up today for the trial.

"It is true," Carol said.

Her husband rose to his feet next to her, his face red and flustered.

"Carol! What are you doing?"

Carol signaled for him to be quiet. "You can't stop me now, John."

Wanton's lawyer then stood up, looking at the judge. "Your Honor, this is highly unusual. As Richard Wanton's repre..."

"I'll allow it," Judge Moore said.

"But Your Honor, this has nothing to do with..."

"I said, I'll allow it. I want to hear it. Continue, Mrs. Savage."

"Thank you, Your Honor," Carol said and looked at her husband, who had sat back down. "It's true what Mrs. Thomas is saying. These past several years, I have watched what you and Richard Wanton did to these women and how you threatened them to silence. Often, it took place in my own home, and I would see the girls storm out, crying helplessly. I finally had enough. So, I decided to find them—one after the other. I went through your personal computer and found their names and addresses. Now, I have gathered them all and recorded their stories. I have even brought some of them here today."

Carol Savage turned to look at the crowd behind her.

"Stand up, girls. Please."

Silence went through the room, and nothing happened. Everyone looked at one another until suddenly, a woman in the far back rose to her feet.

"H-hello. My name is Victoria. I was r-raped by Richard Wanton in 2002 in his apartment. He told me he could get me the position of a weather girl."

Three seats to her right, another woman stood up, holding onto the back of the chair in front of her. "My name is Lisa. I was lured into Richard Wanton's apartment in March 2005 for a job interview, where he and his anchor Mitt Paige told me I had to sleep with them both to get the job. So, I did."

Two rows in front of her, a red-haired woman got up. "Hello. My name is Michelle. I was told that I had to give Wanton a blowjob in his office, or he'd ruin my career."

Another deep silence went through the room, and Rachel felt her hands get clammy.

Then, she stood up too.

Heart hammering in her chest, panic threatening to erupt.

"Hello."

She stopped and cleared her throat while calming her beating heart. Her entire body was screaming for her to run away, to hide. But she didn't. She calmed the voices down, then did exactly what she had come for.

She spoke up:

"H-hello. My name is Rachel. I was raped by Wanton and his friend in 2010 in Wanton's apartment. I let the abuse define me. For years, I told myself it was all I was—that I should be ashamed of myself. That I had failed, made a mistake, and now I was paying the price. I was guilty, dirty. I told myself I had to behave. I had to be a good girl because I was ashamed of myself. Do you know what that does to a woman? To feel such deep shame and disgust with the very person you are? But not anymore. Now, I am redefining myself. I am changing the way I see it, how I see myself. That is why I am speaking up today. Thank you."

After finishing, Rachel kept standing, barely breathing, her heart still beating so fast it seemed like it would never calm down again.

A woman in front of her rose from her seat, turned to face her, and began to clap. Several other women joined her, and soon the entire room was standing and clapping. Wanton's lawyers were protesting, trying to get the judge to stop it, but the loud cheering and clapping drowned them out.

"There, you have it," Carol said when it died down. "I have gathered more than fifty women who are ready to speak up now, and I have recorded all their stories. Most of them have not only gone through abuse but also had to deal with being threatened into silence afterward. It's all recorded in their stories. It should be enough to take both Wanton and Paige down for years."

"No one will listen to your crazy stories," Wanton said with a huff, puffing himself up. "I'm a free man. You can't stop me from walking out of here. Your Honor, will you dismiss the case?"

Judge Moore looked at him above his glasses, then said:

"I don't have any other choice. Case dismissed."

As the gavel fell, Wanton grabbed his jacket and walked out triumphantly, winking at Rachel as he passed her.

Chapter 80

"Like I told you from the beginning. I didn't kill that woman. Now, I have the court's word for it. It was all a lie."

"Does that mean you're a free man?" the reporter asked.

"Yes, I am fully acquitted. The truth was finally brought to the light of day."

I walked past Richard Wanton on the stairs of the courthouse, where he was talking to the hundreds of reporters that had attacked him as soon as he walked out. Isabella was right next to me. She saw the look on my face, then smiled.

"Let him gloat. It won't be for long."

"I just hate to see him go free," I said.

She nodded. "As I said. He won't be a free man for long."

She lifted the file that Carol Savage had handed to her, then tapped the top of it. "We've got a pretty strong case here. Once Carol gets me the recordings, we'll get him. Justice will be served."

"I sure hope so, for the sake of those poor women. It took some guts to stand up in there today."

"It won't be wasted," Isabella said as we moved onto the pavement. Miranda, Tristan, and Kimmie were waiting there for me. "You know it won't. With what you have provided us, we'll even get Savage too for hiring assassins to come after you and Kimmie and blackmailing a federal agent, which leads me to you. How are you holding up? It took some pretty big guts to do what you did today as well. And these past several days, making sure Kimmie was safe. I prayed you'd make it to the trial in time, but I have to say I almost lost hope in there. I tried to stall everything as long as I could."

"Putting out a warrant for my arrest to let me know you knew I had Kimmie was quite clever. I almost missed it, thinking you had it in for me."

She gave me a look. "Really? You know me better than that."

"Yeah," I said and punched her lovingly on the shoulder. "That's how I figured it out. I realized you had no other choice, no other way of contacting me without the leak finding out."

"I knew you would get it."

"And Timmy? What will happen?"

"He'll have to hand in his badge. He'll be prosecuted for having sex with a minor, of course. Then it's up to the higher powers—my superiors—to determine if he will be prosecuted as well for obstructing the investigation and endangering a witness. It doesn't look good for him, to be honest. But we'll have to wait and see. That's none of your concern. I'll take it from here. Go home, Eva Rae. Go home to your children and hold them a little tighter."

I hugged her, then waved and went back to the others. Kimmie and Tristan were waiting for a taxi to take them back to their own home. I still had to go back to the farm and get my bag before I'd grab the first plane home to Cocoa Beach. Miranda held up the keys to her truck. It was parked on the side of the street farther down the road, where we had left it when rushing to the courthouse earlier.

"You ready?"

I nodded, then paused. "Just give me a second."

I rushed toward Kimmie, who was waiting by the curb, then grabbed her from behind and hugged her.

"What was that for?" she asked.

"That was my way of saying I forgive you," I said. "For everything."

"Are you going soft on me, Eva Rae?" she asked, grinning. She went serious. "Thank you, though. It means more than you think. Now, I might begin the process of forgiving myself for it too. For that and so much more."

I placed a hand on her shoulder and squeezed it.

"You're all right, Kick-ass Kimmie."

That made her laugh. "See you around, Eva Rae."

"Probably not, but let's leave it at that," I said, then waved at her and Tristan and hurried back to Miranda. I looked over my shoulder at Kimmie as I reached the purple truck, then wondered for a brief second if circumstances had been different if I could have been friends with her.

THE END

Afterword

Dear Reader,

Thank you for purchasing and reading *Such a Good Girl* (Eva Rae Thomas #9).

This was by far the hardest and most personal book I ever had to write. I can't believe I actually did it.

Big parts of this book are my own story. I have been dealing with this for the past year and felt it needed to be told.

It all began when I was contacted by a journalist from Denmark, who was doing a documentary about sexual harassment in the Danish media.

She contacted me because my name kept coming up during her research. I used to be a reporter at a prominent national TV network and was also an anchor for a period of time before moving to the States, where I started writing books.

When the journalist contacted me, I hadn't thought about any of those old stories for twenty years.

Suddenly, it was all I could think about. It came back to me in these violent flashbacks that completely floored me. Just like Rachel in this book, I found myself crying for entire days and unable to function properly. I had repressed this for so long; I had almost completely forgotten it. But now, it was back, and it almost knocked me out. I couldn't eat, I couldn't sleep, but worst of all, I couldn't write, and that's what I love to do.

I spoke to a therapist, and she told me I needed to talk about it. I had to go through a healing process, and part of it was talking about it.

So, I finally told my story. First to my loved ones, then to some lawyers, and finally to the journalist while on camera.

A few months later, two of the three men involved were fired from the network. One of them was the most prolific anchor our nation has ever had, so it was a big story back home. We all grew up with him, watching him deliver the news or be funny on quiz shows, and now he had his own talk show.

Until he was fired. Because of my story that is similar to Samantha's in this book. It also happened while I was an intern, but I never told anyone. I decided to hide it away because I was so embarrassed and blamed myself.

The last guy who became the news director back then doesn't work at the network anymore but is an editor-in-chief of a big newspaper, so nothing has so far happened to him.

But the documentary hasn't even been aired yet. It will be soon, and then we'll see what happens.

I am super nervous about when it does since the entire country will know my story, but I also know that telling my story is important, and hopefully, it will help someone else to stand up for themselves.

Maybe it can hinder this from happening to more women.

As usual, I want to thank you for all your continuous support and remind you to leave a review if possible. It means so much to me.

Take care,

Willow

About the Author

Willow Rose is a multi-million-copy best-selling Author and an Amazon ALL-star Author of more than 80 novels. Her books are sold all over the world.

She writes Mystery, Thriller, Paranormal, Romance, Suspense, Horror, Supernatural thrillers, and Fantasy.

Willow's books are fast-paced, nail-biting page-turners with twists you won't see coming. That's why her fans call her The Queen of Plot Twists.

Several of her books have reached the Kindle top 10 of ALL books in the US, UK, and Canada. She has sold more than three million books all over the world.

Willow lives on Florida's Space Coast with her husband and two daughters. When she is not writing or reading, you will find her surfing and watch the dolphins play in the waves of the Atlantic Ocean.

Tired of too many emails? Text the word: "willowrose" to 31996 to sign up to Willow's VIP Text List to get a text alert with news about New Releases, Giveaways, Bargains and Free books from Willow.

CPSIA information can be obtained
at www.ICGtesting.com
Printed in the USA
BVHW031643170621
609824BV00001B/54

9 781954 938199